CASE WITHOUT A CORPSE

CASE WITHOUT A CORPSE

By

LEO BRUCE

Academy
Chicago

First American Edition 1982 Academy Chicago

Published by Academy Chicago
425 North Michigan Ave.
Chicago, IL 60611

Printed and bound in the U.S.A.

First paperback edition 1982 Academy Chicago

Library of Congress Cataloging in Publication Data

Bruce, Leo, 1903–1980.
    Case without a corpse.

    Reprint. Originally published: London: G. Bles, 1937.
    I. Title
PR6005.R673C38   1982   823′.912   82–3916
ISBN 0–89733–052–8   AACR2
ISBN 0–89733–050–1 (pbk.)

PART ONE

CHAPTER I

IT was, I shall have to admit, a dark and stormy night. I have always thought it odd that so many crimes have taken place to the accompaniment of howling winds and nightmare tempests. It is odd, but not altogether unaccountable, for they are the supremely right accompaniment. And when I look back on the affair which reached its climax that evening, I realize that the weather could not well have been otherwise.

I was staying at Braxham, a country town in one of the home counties. Actually, I like country towns. Most people say dogmatically that they must either have "the real country" or London itself. They affect to find places like Braxham— or Horsham, or Ashford, or Chelmsford or East Grinstead—provincial and dull. But I disagree. There is just enough population to form a self-contained world, and in that world surprising things take place which never reach the London Press, and types and characters develop freely, and situations become tense, and life has a dramatic way of twisting itself about. And it is all visible, audible, notable—the ideal theatre for any one like me, who wants to see things happen.

But I had another reason for staying at Braxham. My old friend Sergeant Beef, after his unexpected solution of the Thurston murder,[1] had been promoted to this larger area. And on the evening in question, Wednesday, February 22nd, I was actually in his excellent company in the public bar of the Mitre.

Now Sergeant Beef was essentially a country policeman. His red-veined face and straggling ginger moustache, his slow movements and deliberate and plodding manner of thought, stamped him as one of those irritating rustic individuals on bicycles who stop your car without apparent provocation, to see whether you have got a mirror. His dialect, too, the mixed and curious Cockney of the districts outside London, was not calculated to assist his promotion in a Force over-run by zestful public school boys, and gentlemen trained at the police college. But there was his record. From the time he had joined the Force, a gaping, ginger-haired youth, until now that he was in his late forties, he had never, it was said, "missed his man." Whether it had been a stolen bicycle in the Sussex village he had ruled, or the murder of a doctor's wife, as in his most recent case, Sergeant Beef had stolidly but relentlessly applied the simple principles of detection he had learnt, and eventually made his arrest. With everything else against him, he had been too successful to pass over, so that here he was, in charge, at the quite important little town of Braxham.

I, personally, was delighted. The Sergeant, for me, represented most that was worth while in the English character. He appeared almost

[1] See *The Case for Three Detectives.*

a fool, he was slow and independent, he was quite fearless, and his imagination was of the kind which did not appear till he took an important step. He loved a game and a glass, and he had the awed interest that Englishmen often have in the slick and sinister cleverness of the outwardly brilliant. And he always got there in the end.

That evening he was in mufti, playing darts. Already, I gathered, there had been murmurs in the town that the new Sergeant—he had been at Braxham for a year or more, but he was still "new" there—spent too much of his time in local pubs. The Vicar was quite concerned about it, and talked of "a bad example." There had even been a complaint to the Chief Constable. But Beef went his way. He never, he maintained, neglected his duty, and how he spent his free evenings was his own affair.

He was a passionate dart-player. I use the adjective deliberately. To watch that solid and solemn man standing before the little round board with the three darts in his hand, preparing to score his final double, was a revelation. His glazed eyes were awakened, his impassive face was lit. He was immensely happy. And yet he was no champion. He "played a decent game," people said. He "could hold his own." But his style wasn't spectacular. It was his fervour that was remarkable, not his skill.

That evening he and I had been partners against Fawcett, the postman, and Harold, the publican's son. They had come in early, for the wind and rain which lashed the street had to be faced, and they had wanted to get the walk done with, so that they could settle down by the inn fire. The little public bar was inviting, clean and warm, and the dripping overcoats and umbrellas hanging near the door were visibly steaming.

Sergeant Beef and I had lost the first game, and my partner was not pleased. There was a lull in the play while we paid for the customary drinks, and as if to smooth over the slightly irritated atmosphere, Fawcett began to talk.

"I see young Rogers is home again," he said.

Sergeant Beef grunted. It was evident that he did not like "young Rogers."

"Shouldn't mind having *his* job," Fawcett continued.

"What is it?" I asked.

"He's a steward on one of the liners that go to South America. He gets very good money." Then, turning to Sergeant Beef, he said grinning—"Going to run him in this time, Sergeant?"

Beef, appealed to in his professional capacity, answered in the pompous voice he kept for such moments. "If 'e does anything wot calls for it," he said, "'e will be arrested." And he swallowed the rest of his beer.

Fawcett winked to me. "Regular young rascal, this Rogers," he explained. "Always up to something. Last time he was home the Sergeant had him up for being drunk and disorderly.

And it's not the first time he's been in trouble."

"Local boy?" I asked.

"He's not so much of a boy. Thirty-five or six, I should say. He's a nephew of Mr. Rogers, the bootmaker, in the High Street. They've only lived here about five years."

"And he's the black sheep of the town?" I suggested.

"He's a real bad hat," said Fawcett. "Not just one of your happy-go-luckies. Why, I could tell you things about him, if we wasn't in the hearing of the Law!" He nodded with a grin at the back of Sergeant Beef. "But his old aunt and uncle's crazy about 'im. They won't hear nothing against him. And he plays them up, of course. Decent old people, they are. It's a shame. But he'll come a cropper one of these days."

The publican, a Mr. Simmons, leaned over the bar. "He was in here to-day," he said, "not long before we closed at half-past two. He came in with that Fairfax, who stays at the Riverside Hotel."

"That chap who comes down for the fishing?"

"That's him. They came in together, him and young Rogers."

"Go on!" said Fawcett, not very interested but feigning surprise.

"Yes. I couldn't help noticing because while they were in here a foreigner came in."

"A foreigner?" said Beef. All foreigners to him were obviously suspect. "What sort of a foreigner?"

"I didn't like the look of him," said Mr. Simmons. "Dark, he was. Might have been half Indian. He couldn't speak a lot of English."

"There you are!" said Fawcett.

"Well, as soon as young Rogers and Fairfax saw this fellow, they drank up and went out. I shouldn't have noticed it, only when they'd gone the foreigner turned round to me and asks Fairfax's name."

"That's funny," admitted Beef. "Did 'e say any more?"

"No. He was gone in a minute. Almost as though he had gone after them, it was."

"I never much cared for foreigners myself," said Beef. And a moment later we were listening to war-time stories, calculated to rouse our distaste for foreigners of all sorts. However, this topic was exhausted in time, and was followed by a lull, in which the noise of the storm outside was unpleasantly noticeable.

Soon we started to play the return match on the dart-board. Our backs were to the door, and though there were several entrances behind us while we played, we scarcely turned to see who had come in. The game was too exciting.

It must have been about twenty past eight when, in the final "leg," Sergeant Beef required only the double eighteen to win the match. Harold had left his partner the double top, on which Fawcett was almost a certainty, so that if the Sergeant missed this time the game was lost.

"Well, I'm going to try for it," he announced as he took the darts out of Harold's hand.

There was a breathless silence. Sergeant Beef stood firmly on his heels, and prepared to throw. Every one in the bar had turned to see him. I was as tense as if my whole future hung on this, and I could see the Sergeant's eyes alight with excitement.

It was at this point that the street door opened, and someone entered and said, "Sergeant!"

Beef did not turn round, but growled, "'Arf a minute, can't you? I'm 'aving my turn."

He threw the first of his darts. It was outside the line—a quarter of an inch away.

"Sergeant!" This time the voice was loud and insistent. "I've come to give myself up. I've committed a murder."

Quicker than any of us, Sergeant Beef spun round. "That's different," he said.

We found ourselves staring towards the door, just inside which stood the man who, as I afterwards learnt, was called "young Rogers." He was hatless, and the rain streamed down his face from his dark hair, while the shoulders of his suit were soaked. He was rather white as he looked across at us.

Then, before any of us could move, he pulled out a small bottle, and, throwing his head back, swallowed the contents. There was a brief pause, then his body seemed to give one agonised spasm and he dropped with a double thud to the floor.

We rushed forward, but Sergeant Beef was the first to examine him. He tugged at his collar and opened it. The publican came hurrying round with a glass of water. But Beef, who had thrust his hand in to the fellow's heart, looked up.

"Dead as mutton," he said, and rose to his feet.

CHAPTER II

WHILE we still stood over the dead man the door was pushed open again. Previously there had been no gush of wind, for everyone who had entered had closed the door from the passage into the street before entering the bar. But this time a cold, wet blast came with the new arrival.

It was a girl. I saw her face, and though I could not be certain (for her cheeks were wet with rain), I thought that she was crying already before she saw young Rogers on the floor. She was a handsome girl, slim, blonde, delicate. She wore a wet mackintosh and gloves, and a small, rain-soaked hat.

"Alan!" she cried, and dropped to her knees beside the young man. Then—"Is he dead?" she whispered, looking up to us who stood about her.

Sergeant Beef nodded. And now there was no doubt about the girl's tears. She pressed her wet face to his and sobbed, quite unconscious of our embarrassment.

Even in the stress of those moments I was aware of a strong sense of curiosity. Would the apparently phlegmatic Sergeant rise to the occasion? How would my village policeman deal with a man who had confessed to murder and poisoned himself, and a girl sobbing over his dead body? Personally I should have been completely at a loss. But then I am anything but a man of action.

Sergeant Beef stood straight up, sucked his moustache, cleared his throat and began. "'Arold," he said to the publican's son, "would you be kind enough to go and fetch Dr. Little?" At any other time, there would have been no 'would you be kind enough' but on these occasions the Sergeant's verbiage grew weighty. "And Mr. Simmons, I'll ask you to close this bar till the doctor arrives. If you gentlemen would be good enough. . . ." And he began to clear the room.

I was staying in the house, and felt privileged to remain behind. The Sergeant now turned to the sobbing girl.

"Now, Miss Cutler," he said, "come along. Mrs. Watt will take you home. This isn't the place for you. You can't do nothink for 'im."

At first she took no notice, but when Sergeant Beef touched her arm and insisted again, she looked up.

"How did it happen?" she murmured.

"You'll hear all about it in good time. Now come along, Miss. Mrs. Watt is waiting to take you home."

Quite kindly, but forcefully, he helped the girl to her feet, and led her to Mrs. Watt who was waiting in the passage. Then, alone in the bar with me, he stared down at the dead man.

"Nasty turn-out," he remarked.

"Yes. If only we could have been a bit quicker. . . ."

But Sergeant Beef was on his knees again.

"Gor, look at this," he said, and held up the dead man's right arm. "If that's not 'uman blood, I'm a Dutchman."

There was a stain which I could see now in spite of the wetness of the jacket, while the cuff of the shirt was red, too. Sergeant Beef touched it, looked at his finger, and whistled.

"And it *is* blood, this time," he murmured.

After a few moments' pause he began groping in the side pocket of the dead man's jacket. He had some difficulty in extricating what he found there, but he managed it at last, and showed me a short, ugly-looking knife of the type that sailors carry. This, too, was stained with blood.

"That's wot 'e done it with, I suppose," said Sergeant Beef, and laid it on the wooden bench beside him.

He began to empty the man's pockets. There was a pocket-case containing seventeen one-pound notes, and a photograph of the girl who had just left us. This was signed, "To dearest Alan from Molly," in thin, plain, girlish hand-writing. There was some silver, a packet of cigarettes, a box of matches, and a key-ring. That was all.

"Well," said the Sergeant, "I can't do nothink more till the doctor's had a look at him. I don't know whether you'd mind, sir, giving me an 'and to get 'im off of the floor?"

I nodded, rather unwillingly.

"Mr. Simmons," called Sergeant Beef, "where'd you like 'im put?" He spoke as calmly as if he were delivering a cask of beer.

Mr. Simmons appeared behind the bar. "I don't want him in the house at all," he grumbled.

"Well, of course you don't," said the Sergeant. "And I don't want him in my district at all. But there's some things we can't help, and a corpse is one of them. Now, where'll you 'ave 'im?"

"Better put him along that bench," said the publican, and we at once lifted the corpse, and placed it along the wooden bench indicated.

"I don't know 'ow *you* feel," said Sergeant Beef to me, "but after that job I could do with somethink short. Then I must go and find out 'oo that dam' young fool's done in. Mr. Simmons, I'll 'ave a double Scotch."

I watched him swallow it, and heard him suck his moustache. "Like me to come with you?" I asked.

"No. You better stay here in the warm. I don't suppose I shall be long."

So I settled down beside the fire again. Mr. Simmons, leaning across the counter, grew philosophical after the Sergeant had gone out.

"I knew he was a rackety young chap," he said, "but I never thought it would come to this. Fancy doing anyone in! And then coming here to poison himself. It won't do the house any good, will it? I mean people won't like coming to a place where anyone's likely to be poisoned every five minutes. But still there's the publicity and that. I suppose it'll get into the papers. I mean, you never know what's going to do you harm and what isn't nowadays, do you?"

I said you didn't, noting cynically how the man turned to his own interests.

"I tell you what, though," went on Mr. Simmons, "I wouldn't be a bit surprised if it was that foreigner that he's murdered. You know, the one that came in here to-day."

I had forgotten that. "Why? What makes you think so?" I asked.

His answer was disappointing. "Well, it seems funny, doesn't it? A foreigner we've never seen before asking about him at twenty past two, and at half-past eight he pops up to say he's murdered someone."

"Funny" was not the word I should have chosen, but I nodded. "You may be right," I said, for my interest in crime had already taught me never to jump to conclusions.

Just then the doctor came in, followed by Harold. He was a young, rather good-looking man, this Doctor Little, and he moved confidently, with his hands thrust deep in the pockets of a green ulster.

"Good evening," he said. "Ah, here he is. I'll just have a look at him." He sniffed the air as he approached the dead man.

I'm afraid I was too squeamish to watch the examination, though the publican and his son did so avidly. To tell the truth, I can honestly say that at this point I was not very excited by these events. I liked problems, not a sordid and open case of murder and suicide. I had often wondered whether Sergeant Beef would ever have another opportunity of using his slow but certain wits to solve a crime. It had seemed scarcely likely. Only by an amazing coincidence could more than one murder investigation fall to the lot of a provincial policeman. And now that there had been a murder in his district it was a plain and unpleasant case, in which the murderer had already confessed.

The doctor reported at last. "Cyanide of potassium," he said shortly. "Death must have been almost instantaneous. I'll send up a full report in the morning."

"Doctor, may I introduce myself?" I began. "My name's Townsend."

"How d'you do? Have a drink?"

"I was just going to ask you. Unpleasant business, this."

He shrugged. I had the impression that he was trying to appear a more practised and blasé person than he was. "I had a dinner-party," he said, "and was playing bridge when the boy came for me."

I refrained from retaliating with my interrupted game of darts. "Did you know young Rogers?" I asked instead.

"I've seen him about," said the doctor. "Crazy young fellow. He nearly knocked me down this morning on that motor-bike of his. Well, I must be getting back to my guests."

"You'll probably be wanted again presently," I said, for his pretence at indifference annoyed me.

"Why? You thinking of doing the same thing?"

"No. But you evidently don't know why

young Rogers took poison. He had committed a murder."

"Good Lord!"

I was pleased to see that I had made an impression at last. "Yes. And Sergeant Beef is finding out whom he has murdered. As soon as he's done so, I suppose they'll call on you again."

"Yes. Blast them. I suppose they will. Unless by any luck it wasn't in Braxham."

"But . . ."

"He was on that motor-bike to-day, remember."

I had not thought of that. The doctor smiled, nodded, and went out.

"Seems to know *his* way about," I remarked to Mr. Simmons.

"Yes. He thinks a bit of himself. But he's a fine doctor. He saved young Harold's life last year. Treats everyone the same — panel or not. And he always comes when you need him."

Mr. Simmons left me, for it was ten o'clock, and he had to close his doors. Murder or no murder, that was a matter which could not be neglected. If half the inhabitants of Braxham had taken cyanide of potassium it would have made no difference. Closing hour was the most respected rite in all England. So I reflected somewhat bitterly as I heard his bolts go home.

I was conscious of feeling very tired. The events of the last hour had been startling and gruesome enough to take all the life out of me. I wanted to get to bed, and forget the white face of young Rogers as he had stood in front of us, waiting to make an end of himself before our very eyes. I wanted to get the recollection of that knife out of my brain. I decided that to-morrow I would leave Braxham and return to London, where, if such things happened, one was not made aware of them.

I went into the sitting-room of the inn, where Mrs. Simmons brought my supper. But the sight of the underdone beef was revolting to me, and I could not eat. I lit a cigarette, and waited. I felt that I could not very well go to bed till Sergeant Beef returned. But I did not encourage Mrs. Simmons, a short, trim, respectable person with glasses, to discuss the matter with me as she cleared away.

At last, about eleven o'clock, there was a knocking on the side-door, and Sergeant Beef was with us.

"Most extraordinary thing," he said. "No one's missing, that I can hear of. I've telephoned everywhere. Sent round to every house he's known at. Not a sign of nothink. The police all round think I'm barmy, ringing up and arsking for a corpse."

He was out of breath and out of temper.

"I don't know," he said. "I always supposed a murder case started with a corpse, and then you had to find out 'oo done it. This time we know oo's done it, but we can't find the corpse. Wot d'you say to that?"

"I think it's early to say anything, Sergeant. The corpse may be out in the woods, or anywhere."

"But no one's been missed," grumbled the Sergeant.

"Nor was there in the Brighton Trunk Murder, till they found the body, then there were hundreds. You wait till the morning. You'll soon find out whom he killed."

"D'you know," returned Sergeant Beef, unexpectedly. "This 'ere's too much for me. This 'ere's a case for Scotland Yard. And what's more I'm going to ring 'em up."

CHAPTER III

I was frankly disappointed. I remembered how Sergeant Beef had loftily dismissed the suggestion that he should call in "the Yard" in the Thurston mystery, and it seemed like pusillanimity on his part now. And it was surely premature. The murder, it appeared, had been committed only a few hours ago, and the fact that his telephone calls had failed to reveal anyone as missing, or to give him information of a discovered corpse, meant nothing at all.

"Well," I said, "you know your business best, but I really can't understand you giving up already."

Sergeant Beef eyed me somewhat beerily. "I 'aven't give up," he said, "I don't say I shan't get to the bottom of this, like I 'ave of other myst'ries. Only last week there was a bit of a 'ow-d'ye-do at the Church 'ere. Someone 'ad been after the alms-boxes. I got 'er, though. It turned out to be the woman wot swep' up on Mondays, 'oo 'ad said she'd seen a tall man walking mysterious down the aisle. I got 'er already. And I don't say I shan't get at the truf of this. But I know my duty. When there's feachers in a case wot seems extraordinary, it's my job to inform Scotland Yard. Well? Aren't there 'ere? 'Ave you ever 'eard of a murder where you know 'oo the murderer is and can't

find out 'oo 'e's murdered? Corse you 'aven't.
I don't believe it's ever 'appened before. And
if that's not extraordinary feachers I don't know
wot is. So I shall ring 'em up first thing."

But there was one more interruption that
night before we could go to bed. While Sergeant
Beef was fumbling with the buttons of his overcoat there was a knock at the door, not very
loud, but distinctly audible in the back room
where we stood.

Simmons turned to the Sergeant. He was
angry now. "I don't see why this house should
be turned into a police-station. I want to get
to bed."

"Can't be 'elped," said Beef lethargically. "I
didn't choose where 'e was to do 'isself in. Will
you go and see 'oo it is, or shall I?"

Mr. Simmons left us, and we could hear the
sound of the bolts withdrawn.

"Is Sergeant Beef here?" came an anxious
male voice.

"Yes, Mr. Rogers. Come inside." Simmons's
voice had lost its roughness. "Put your umbrella
down there. Still raining I see."

"Where is the Sergeant?" The voice was
querulously impatient.

We heard the two men approaching, and I
turned to examine "old Mr. Rogers." He wasn't
really so old—in his late fifties, I judged. He
was a small man, with a little straggling and
dishevelled grey hair on the sides of his head,
and watery weak eyes. His clothes were baggy,
and his appearance rather that of a worried,
fussy, elderly rabbit. I wondered if he already

knew about his nephew, and disliked the thought of his hearing the story now. In spite of my interest in human nature, I always find an emotional climax embarrassing. But with his first words he put my mind at rest on this point.

"The constable has been round to tell me, Sergeant," he said.

"Yes. We're very sorry about it, Mr. Rogers."

He seemed scarcely to know that Beef had spoken. There was evidently something else on his mind. He looked up at us a minute, then down to the thick green table-cloth. I saw that he was trembling.

"My wife . . ." he whispered at last.

Beef jumped up. He moved more quickly than I thought possible for him.

"Your wife? Not . . ."

Mr. Rogers shrugged. Then he pulled a telegram from his pocket, and handed it to Sergeant Beef.

"This came to-day," he said, "I've never known her to do such a thing before. If you knew my wife you would understand that it . . . that I can't believe. . . ." His eyes dropped again. "Sergeant," he said suddenly, "Do you think it could have anything to do with . . . ?" He was quite incoherent, yet we could understand well enough what he was suggesting.

Sergeant Beef was still staring at the telegram. "Sent off from ——" he said, naming the London station from which the main line ran to Braxham, "at 12.15. Did you know she was going to London?"

"Oh yes, Sergeant. She went up on a Day
Return. I've been down to the station and
asked. She took a day return as she always did.
She was going to get a little present for . . ."
His voice broke.

"I see. The telegram says *Staying night with
friends, returning* 11.15 *a.m. to-morrow.* Wot friends
would that be?"

"I've no idea. That's the extraordinary part.
We had a few friends in Bromley where we used
to live. But we haven't seen them for years.
And I've *never* known her to stay away for a
night. And with young Alan home. . . ."

"'E didn't go up with 'er yesterday, I suppose?"

"He was away all day. He had his motor-bike.
I don't know where he was till he came
and . . ."

"'E told you wot 'e'd done?"

Mr. Rogers nodded. "It was about eight
o'clock," he said, "when he came back. He was
muddy up to the eyes. All his motor-biking
things was wet and dirty. I could see as soon as
he came into the room that there was something
wrong. 'Wot is it, Alan?' I asked him. He
looked at me stupidly for a minute, then he said,
'Uncle . . . I've committed a murder.'"

"And you believed him at once?"

"Well, yes. It was the way he looked, and
that. He was half crazy. I just said 'Who?'
like that. But he shook his head, and wouldn't
answer. Then I thought that p'raps he had not
really killed anyone, only believed he had. So I
said, 'Best thing you can do is to go and give

yourself up.' I somehow thought that he couldn't have done anything in cold blood. There would be provocation, or something. I was already thinking how we should go about getting him off. You see, he'd often been in scrapes before. He'd been to me many times to own up to something he had done. And we'd always managed to get him out of it. It never occurred to me that we shouldn't have a try this time. Only if . . . if it could be anything to do with his auntie. . . ."

"Can you think of any reason why 'e might have gone for 'er?"

"Reason? There could be no reason, unless he was out of his mind. She's done everything for him."

"Well, Mr. Rogers, I don't see that there's any cause for you to go connecting the two. We'll trace both of their movements to-morrow. I expect you'll find Mrs. Rogers coming 'ome as right as rain in the morning. No reason why she *shouldn't* stay in London if she wanted. . . ."

"But she's never thought of such a thing before. . . ."

"No. Well. Don't you get anythink into your 'ead too soon. Mustn't go jumping to conclusions. Doesn't do in a turn-out like this. I shall 'ave to come along and arsk you all sorts of questions in the morning, about your nephew, and that. And by then I expect your wife'll be 'ome as right as a trivet. Now the best thing you can do is to go along and get some sleep. . . ."

"Sleep?" Mr. Rogers groaned as though he

did not understand what sleep was. "With all this?"

"I know it's a narsty shock for you. Your nephew and one thing and another." The Sergeant was trying to be soothing. "Still—there you are. And worrying your 'ead off won't 'elp you."

Suddenly a new idea seemed to come to the little man. "But—haven't you found out? Isn't anyone missing? You haven't found anything to tell you who it was that Alan . . . ?"

Beef shook his head. "Nothink 'asn't come to light as yet," he said. "But it will, in due course."

"It's terrible for me," moaned Mr. Rogers.

"Now come along," said the Sergeant, and clumsily took his arm. "You've got to get some rest."

Obediently, but with a sort of vague looseness, Mr. Rogers walked towards the door.

"Good night, Mr. Rogers," someone called. But he went out without answering.

Mr. Simmons yawned. But this new development had awakened my curiosity.

"Do you really think it could be the old lady?" I asked Beef.

"I never jump to conclusions," said the Sergeant sternly. "Nor vencher an opinion when there's not sufficient evidence. And now, gentlemen. . . ."

CHAPTER IV

BUT before the Sergeant could leave us Mr. Simmons addressed him.

"Are you going to leave him in the bar all night?" he asked.

There was no need for Simmons to explain what was referred to as "him."

"Don't see why not," said Beef.

"Oh, you don't? Well, I do," returned Simmons truculently. "It's bad enough having a dead 'un in the house all night, without everyone who uses the bar knowing afterwards that it was there all the time. Besides, even if the chap is a murderer and suicide and that, he's dead. And it's not respectful to the dead to leave them in a public. And how's young Harold to go about sweeping the place up in the morning?"

As though convinced by these arguments Beef rose. "Wot you want done with 'im then?"

"I'd like you to take him away altogether."

"Wot, wheel 'im on my bicycle, I suppose?" suggested Beef indignantly. "I'd like to know what more you want. P'raps you expect me to take 'im to bed with me?"

"Well, surely there's somewhere for him? What on earth do we pay taxes for?"

Beef looked stern. "It can 'ardly be expected that the authorities are to build a special mortuary in Braxham. It's not every day we get a suicide, nor yet a murder."

"It's a good thing we don't," returned Simmons, "if they're going to choose my hotel to do it in. Well, if you can't take him away he better be put in the club-room at the back."

Beef nodded, and the two men approached the corpse. When they had lifted it, I went to open the door into the private part of the house, through which they could reach the club-room. But Simmons detained me.

"Not that way," he said, "Mrs. Simmons is still up, and we don't want to run into her with it. Might give her a bad turn. We must take him round outside."

So I opened the two doors into the street, and Beef and Simmons brought their burden through.

It was while they were carrying it down the few yards of pavement to the door through which they would pass into the Mitre yard, that I observed someone watching the whole procedure. He was immediately noticeable, for at that time of night in Braxham there was nobody about. It gave me quite a start to see him standing on the other side of the road, his hands in the pockets of his overcoat, and a black hat pulled rather far forward. He did not move when we came out, but I could see that he was watching closely. I don't know even now quite what gave me the impression that he was a foreigner. It may have been his black hat and sallow face, or the precise cut of his clothes. But I know that afterwards when I remembered him it was with that notion—a silent, motionless, foreign observer of our doings.

In the club-room, after the two had laid the body of young Rogers on a rickety sofa, I turned to Beef.

"Did you see that man?" I asked.

"Wot man?"

"That man on the other side of the road, watching us?"

"No. Just now, d'you mean?"

"Yes. Yes. Out there!"

Beef started off as quickly as he could and Simmons and I followed him. But when we had crossed the yard and come out on to the pavement again there was no sign of the lonely watcher. Beef hurried down to the corner of the road, and looked in all directions, but no one was in sight.

"You must have been seeing things," he said.

"Oh no. He was there all right. No mistake about that. A foreign-looking chap."

"Foreign-looking, eh?" said Beef.

"I wonder if he was the one that came into the bar to-day when Rogers and Fairfax went out," Simmons suggested, as he turned to lock up the club-room and the yard.

"Well, anyway, we can't do no more to-night," said Beef. "It's time we was all in bed. Good night, Mr. Simmons. Night, Mr. Townsend."

And this time he managed to make his departure without further delay.

I went up to bed not altogether pleased with what Beef and Simmons had just done, for the club-room was directly under my own bed-room. But I was so tired that even my proximity to that corpse could not keep me awake, and it cannot have been more than ten minutes after leaving Simmons that I drifted into a deep and satisfying sleep.

Waking up during the night is unusual with me, and when it happens it comes from some outside cause. I remember that I found myself staring at the square of the window, a visible yellow outline due to the street-lamp below. At first I supposed that it was morning, and then had that curious sense of being still deep in the small hours. I turned over, and determined to sleep again.

But no. At first almost negligible, then more insistently, came a sound from below me. A slight thud, I think, though I was too nearly asleep still to be certain. Then a vague rumour of movement.

Perhaps, I thought, it was morning. Perhaps someone was already astir, cleaning the rooms downstairs. I am not an early riser, and had no idea how light or dark it would be at the time the work of the house began. I groped for my watch on the table beside my bed, and looked at its luminous dial. Three o'clock. Then it could scarcely be a dream.

I listened, trying to persuade myself that it was nothing. But that was impossible. The sound was not definable, but there certainly was a sound.

Suddenly I found myself fully awake. Here and now, if ever in my life, was my chance.

Someone had entered the club-room where the corpse of young Rogers lay. Perhaps his object was to steal something from it. Perhaps he meant to remove the body itself. Whatever his plan, he must be prevented and identified. Catching him would, probably clear up the whole mystery which faced Beef. And to me had been given the opportunity of actually contributing something to the investigation.

I slipped quietly from my bed, and pulled on a dressing-gown. I wondered whether to put shoes on. Being without them would give one a feeling of unprotectedness, but wearing them would make one's approach noisy. I left them behind, slowly and silently crossed the room, and got safely to the landing. Then I started to go downstairs.

It is not often that the mere chronicler of crime gets a thrill. His work is usually to attend, as unintelligently as possible, the dreary post-mortems, and to listen, without too much acumen, to the elucidation offered by the masters. But during those few minutes I knew all the excitements of the chase. I was about to do my own part—and an important part it would be.

My imagination played some curious tricks. Before I opened the door I was prepared to find that the dead had risen, that young Rogers himself had left that rickety sofa and was facing me across the room. I myself had seen his livid face, and touched his stone cold flesh, and knew with absolute security that he was dead. But at three o'clock in the morning, roused from sleep by a noise in the room where his corpse lay, I was prepared to believe anything.

I had my hand on the knob of the club-room door, and began, very gently, to turn it. I did not know exactly where the switch of the electric light was, but when I began to push the door open I saw that there would be enough light from the street lamp to see across the room. Suddenly I pushed the door wide open, and looked in.

The lace curtains in front of the window were blowing into the room, and the window was wide open, but no one was in sight. I found the light switch and used it, and the strong electric light failed to reveal any more. On the sofa the corpse seemed undisturbed, and I crossed to it, and pulled back the rug. Young Rogers lay as he had done when we left him. I turned away, feeling rather disturbed.

Only the open window was unusual. I went across to it and looked out on the street. There was no one in sight, and the rain blew angrily in as I stood there. I hurriedly pulled the window down, and slipped the catch across.

Someone had been in the room—there could be no doubt of it. But who? And with what object? If they had hoped to get something from the dead man's pockets they had been disappointed, for we had emptied these ourselves in the bar. Perhaps they had had some other object in view, and I had disturbed them.

On the whole I thought it best to telephone to Beef. He wouldn't like being disturbed at this hour, but he ought to know what had happened. I went through into the sitting-room where the instrument was, and quietly, so as not to disturb any of the Simmons family, asked for his number.

I could hear the bell ringing for a long time before there was an answer. Then I heard the Sergeant's voice, sounding blurred and resentful.

"Wha's it?" he asked.

"Beef—this is Townsend. Someone has just broken into the club-room of the Mitre."

"'V'you got 'im?"

"No."

"'Ow d'you know, then?"

"I heard him from my room upstairs and came down. There was no one here, but the window which overlooks the street was open."

"Did Simmons leave it open?"

"Of course he didn't. You were with him when we brought the corpse in."

"That's funny."

I was tired and irritable. "I don't know about its being funny," I said. "I don't see much fun in being woken up at this time of night. What are you going to do?"

"Do? What 'you mean, do?"

"Well. . . ."

It wasn't a very lucid conversation.

"I don't see what I can do. You say 'e's cleared off. What can be done?"

I was about to slam down the receiver in disgust when Beef spoke again.

"Tell you what," he said, as though he had just had an inspiration, "I'll send a constable round. 'E'll look after it. You wait there. . . ."

And before I could answer, he, and not I, had replaced his receiver.

The situation was absurd, but very unpleasant. I did not like to go back to bed till the constable had made his appearance, since he would probably wake the whole household if there was no one there. I felt that my old friend Beef had been given the luck of what might be another big case, and was mis-handling it badly. I was in a sour and angry mood as I waited in that bare room with the corpse of young Rogers for company.

But it was not long before, on going to the window, I saw a young policeman striding down the road. I opened the window again, relieved to find that there was a momentary lull in the rain. I found myself looking at a young, rather handsome, fellow, with the build and features of a boxer.

"Sergeant Beef sent me round, sir," he said.

"Good." And I told him what had happened.

He grinned pleasantly, and one could not imagine that he had just been called from his sleep to face this unpleasant night.

"That's all right, sir," he said. "I'll carry on! You go back to bed."

Which, gladly enough, I did.

CHAPTER V

I AWOKE next morning to find that the rain had ceased and the wind dropped. There was even a feeble attempt at winter sunlight. But when I got down to breakfast, I found Mrs. Simmons walking about on tip-toe, and speaking in whispers. It seemed that she wished to be conscious of a corpse in the house.

Sergeant Beef arrived about ten o'clock, looking very dejected.

"Well?" I asked him as I emptied my last cup of tea, and lit a cigarette.

"I've been on to 'em," he said, "and only got it in the neck for my trouble. It seems as this isn't regarded as anythink out of the way. I got to trace young Rogers's movements yesterday, and find out 'oo 'e's done for."

"I rather thought that view might be taken," I said. "It seemed to me last night that you were getting worked up too soon. After all, it was only yesterday that the murder happened. The corpse *must* come to light. How could he have got rid of it otherwise? Or else you'll hear who's missing."

"P'raps you're right. I 'ope so, anyway. On'y there's several things I don't like about the 'ole business. Why didn't young Rogers say 'oo it was 'e'd murdered? 'E'd decided to confess and then poison 'isself. It would 'ave

34

been just as easy for 'im to 'ave said, 'I've killed so-and-so,' as to 'ave just said 'e'd committed a murder, wouldn't it?''

"Well, if it turns out to be his aunt, it's understandable. That would have been too much for him to have admitted."

"I don't believe it was his aunt, some'ow. Anyway, she's due in on the eleven-fifteen, and I'm going down to the station to see if she turns up."

"I'll come with you," I said.

Only last night I had decided to get back to London, and escape the investigation of this all too sordid affair. But after my nocturnal part in it, I couldn't somehow. My curiosity was thoroughly aroused.

We set out from the Mitre and walked through the busy central street of the little town. The Sergeant answered greetings in an almost surly manner—he was noticeably out of spirits. His liver, I fancied, was not always in the best of conditions during the early morning, and to-day he had not had enough sleep. I glanced aside and saw that his expression was glum, his eyes a trifle bloodshot, and the fringes of his ginger moustache were damp.

On the platform was little Mr. Rogers, pacing impatiently up and down. There were still ten minutes before the train was due, so that he must have arrived early. I thought he looked shabby and pathetic, and he was too preoccupied to notice that he had stepped in a puddle at the further end of the platform. He had not seen us, and Sergeant Beef avoided him, as he made directly for the refreshment room, which had just opened.

"Wot you g't'ave . . ." he asked me.

I had only just finished breakfast, but Beef swallowed a beer gratefully.

"*That's* better!" he sighed, as he laid down the glass.

We went out on to the platform again to see the train approaching from the distance. By the time we reached Mr. Rogers its noise was loud enough to drown his absently mumbled good morning. But before it had stopped we saw a plump, smiling, middle-aged woman waving to him from the window of a third-class carriage.

The little man darted forward. "Madge!" he said before she had had time to descend, "where have you been?"

She was flushed and beaming, as though she had some jolly secret to communicate. "Didn't you get my telegram?"

"Yes, but . . . staying away all night . . . I've been nearly off my head with worry. And something's happened. Something terrible. . . ."

Mrs. Rogers was on the platform now. "What is it, Alf?" Her smile had gone. And when her husband failed to answer. "Something to do with Alan?"

Mr. Rogers nodded. And as though to save us from being present while the painful disclosure was made, Sergeant Beef stepped forward.

"Well, Mr. Rogers," he said, "now as you've

got your good lady back, I'll be trotting along.
I told you she'd be 'ere all right now, didn't
I?" And he and I began to walk away, leaving
the old man to break his tragic news. "I'll
pop round and see you this afternoon," Sergeant
Beef called back, as we made for the ticket-
collector.

After that the Sergeant went back to the
station. He explained that he had a number
of things to do in connection with routine.
He had to make arrangements for the inquest,
he said, and receive reports. He did not intend
to start "the real investigation" until that
afternoon, but he did not see why I shouldn't
be present when he went to take statements.
I thanked him for that concession with a smile.
I knew his weakness for his large notebook,
and guessed that he would like an audience
during his ponderous questioning.

At two o'clock, therefore, we started out.
Beef showed me a formidable list of people whom
he intended to question.

"Always as well to make a list of 'em," he
said, "then you don't forget no one. I remember the time I was investigating all that 'ow-
d'ye-do down in Sussex when they'd pinched
the postmistress's bicycle, it was through someone as I'd clean forgot to put on my list that I
found out about it. Only shows, doesn't it?
Now the first I've got down to-day is that
Molly Cutler wot came tearing into the pub
last night just after young Rogers 'ad poisoned
himself. She lives with 'er mother in an 'ouse
out this way."

The house was semi-detached, but neat and pleasant, with a small square of well-kept garden to it, and fresh white blinds in its windows. The Sergeant marched up to the front door, and rang.

Miss Cutler herself opened it. She was pale and looked wretchedly ill, but she was quite calm.

"Yes," she said, "I expected you, Sergeant. Come in."

She led us to a "front room" in which a bright fire burnt, and there were chairs which looked as though covers had recently been removed from them. In a moment her mother had followed us into the room, a grey-haired person, very neatly dressed, who looked as though she disapproved of most things, but particularly of us.

"Sit down, please," she said coldly. "I should like to be present while you ask my daughter whatever you have to ask her."

Beef was already pulling out his notebook, and according to his habit he came with brutal bluntness to the point.

"Was this young Rogers carrying on with you?" he asked Molly Cutler.

I saw the old lady stiffen, but she said nothing.

"We were engaged," the girl said quietly.

"Secretly engaged," put in her mother, "and without my consent."

"Secretly engaged," repeated Beef, writing laboriously. When his pencil had finished its slow work, he looked up again.

"'Ow long had this been going on?" he asked.

"It was during his last leave that we became engaged. About two months back."

"Did you know of anyone he had a grudge against?"

"No. He wasn't a fellow to bear a grudge."

"No one it would 'ave been in 'is interest to do away with?"

"No."

"There wasn't no other woman, I s'pose?"

Molly Cutler was silent, but her mother broke in. She spoke with a voice in which you could hear suppressed anger against an old grievance. "There most certainly *was* another woman," she said, "and one with whom that reprobate was involved more deeply than he was with my daughter."

Owing to the time it took him to write, Beef's cross-examinations seemed always very protracted. It was thirty seconds before he spoke.

"What was 'er name?" he asked.

"Stella Smythe," said the mother. "He called her an actress, but she was nothing less than a bad woman."

"When did he see her last?"

In answer to that Mrs. Cutler only spoke one word, but it was hissed out with audible venom. And the information it gave was sensational.

"Yesterday!" she said.

"Yesterday? 'Ow d'you know that?" asked Beef, forgetting his solemnity in the excitement of that revelation.

"You tell him, Molly," said the old lady.

The girl began to speak in a toneless voice, as though she knew only too well that she had to tell the story, but had no interest in it any more. "Alan had never deceived me about this girl," she said. "He had known her some years ago in London. And he had once taken her to Chopley for a week-end. That was two years ago. After that he had given her a sum of money, and left her in London. He knew he was wrong, but she was . . . an immoral girl, too. He hoped he would never see her again. He left his ship about that time, and went to work on a different Line. She lost touch with him, I suppose. But it seems that this time she had got to know his ship, and where he lived, and when he got home there was a letter waiting for him, saying that she was coming down to Chopley again, and that if he didn't come and see her, she would come over to his aunt and uncle's house and make a scene. He told me all this quite frankly, and showed me the letter."

While she spoke I watched Molly Cutler, and admired her. Hers was beauty of the rather conventional English type; she had none of the buxom grace so admired by Latins. But her complexion was delicate and lovely, her eyes honest and wide, her whole being almost flower-like. I was sure, too, that she was speaking the truth.

"It was the night before last," she continued, "when he showed me the letter. He said he would go over the next day, that was yesterday, to see her, and settle it once and for all. He said that it was money she wanted. He would give it to her, but he had to be sure that she would not worry us again."

"And did he go?" asked Sergeant Beef.

The girl looked up. "I don't know," she said.

"You never saw him again?"

"Not until last night."

"'Ow was that?"

"We had arranged to meet at seven o'clock."

"Arranged to meet? Why shouldn't 'e come 'ere?"

Mrs. Cutler chimed in again. "The whole thing was being carried on surreptitiously. My daughter knew that it was against my wishes."

"Oh, I see. And where 'ad you arranged to meet at seven o'clock?"

"Outside the Cinema."

A sound like a snort came from Mrs. Cutler, but the girl ignored it. She seemed too proud and too profoundly unhappy to make any retaliation to her mother.

"And 'e never turned up?"

"No."

"'Ow was it you came rushing into the Mitre, then?"

Mrs. Cutler was appalled. "Into the Mitre? Did you really, Molly? I *am* ashamed of you."

"Someone told me later that he had gone there."

"Who told you?"

"A girl I met. Flora Robinson. She saw him go there from his uncle's shop. I . . .

couldn't understand it. I had waited an hour for him that evening. I felt I had to see him at once. I was going to call him out. . . ."

"Not 'ardly wise, that wouldn't 'ave been, Miss," observed Sergeant Beef philosophically. "Men don't never take kindly to being called out of anywhere like that by a woman. . . ."

Mrs. Cutler spoke icily. "Perhaps you will limit your observations to the unpleasant matter in hand," she said.

Beef seemed to remember himself. "Certainly, Ma'am," he said. "And there isn't nothink else you can tell me, Miss Cutler?" he asked.

She shook her head. "I don't think so. Except that whoever Alan has killed it must have been in self-defence, or in a fight or something. It wasn't in his nature to do a cowardly act. Of course, I know you never liked him, Sergeant. . . ."

"Did he tell you that?"

"Yes. He thought you had a down on him. Ever since you arrested him that time."

"Oh, he did."

"Well, that's what he thought. He used to say—of course I don't suppose he meant anything by it—that he'd get his own back on you some day."

"I see. Well, he seems to have done it. He's given me a myst'ry to solve as'll very likely end in my getting into trouble. 'Owever. . . ."

Miss Cutler did not seem to have been listening. "There was one other thing," she said. "He spoke of being followed."

"Followed?" gasped the Sergeant.

"Yes. He didn't give any details, and I thought it was his imagination. But he said he was being followed."

"M'm," said Beef as he picked up his hat, "that's funny." And again, after a long, thoughtful pause, "That's funny."

CHAPTER VI

STRANGELY enough, Sergeant Beef seemed elated by the interview.

"Looks to me," he chuckled, "as though I was right about this, and they was wrong." Beef's "they" always meant his superiors. "This isn't going to be no easy case, after all. We've got the murderer, I admit. But that's not everythink. We've got to find the murder. It's the cart before the 'orse, as you might say."

He was marching along briskly, and our direction was towards Braxham High Street. I did not feel nearly so comfortable about his coming interview with the old couple, for his bludgeoning way of asking questions might hurt them more than he knew. But it was from them that we should probably find out most of "young Rogers'" movements yesterday, and hence make progress.

The shop was closed, and Beef knocked heavily on the door. In a few moments old Rogers stood before us.

"Go easy with Mrs. Rogers, Sergeant," he whispered. "She's taken it very much to heart."

Beef nodded, and all three of us entered a little room behind the shop, where the old lady, who had been so cheerful that morning in the train, sat over the fire with a miserable remnant of wet handkerchief in her hand. Her eyes were swollen with crying.

"Mother thought the world of young Alan," said Mr. Rogers. "She can't believe it of him— not in cold blood, anyway."

She turned towards us. Her voice was shaky, but she seemed to want to express something that she meant very sincerely.

"If there's anything I can tell you that will help to clear this up," she said, "I'll be only too glad. I'm sure when you get to the bottom of it, you'll find our boy only did whatever he has done in self-defence. It couldn't be otherwise."

"Well, first of all I should like to ask you a few questions about yourself, Mrs. Rogers," said Beef unexpectedly. "See, if I've got these notes I took when Mr. Rogers was anxious about you last night, and I'd like to complete them, as it were. You went up to London yesterday, I 'ear?"

"Yes. On the 11.20."

"You took a day return?"

"That's right."

"Meaning to come back last night?"

"Yes. But then I met Mrs. Fairfax in the train. . . ."

"Fairfax?" asked Beef, "I seem to know *that* name. Come from 'ere, does she?"

"Well, she stays down here with her husband now and again."

Beef was beginning his slow scrawl. "What, the gentleman as comes for the fishing? Where do they stay?"

"At the Riverside Private Hotel," said Mrs. Rogers. "He comes down often. But they live in London."

"I see. And you met her in the train. Was she alone?"

"Yes. Her husband was staying on a few days. In the train she suggested that it would be rather a lark for us to go to a theatre last night, and me to stay at their house in Hammersmith. I can't think what made me do it. But at the time there didn't seem anything wrong. I remember she said that it wasn't often we old ones get out on our own. And I used to like a bit of fun. She said we'd go to the Palladium then to the Corner House for supper. I was quite excited about it. So I sent Alf that telegram you saw and off we went."

After the necessary moments of laborious note-taking, Sergeant Beef said, "Why was you going up to London at all that day, Mrs. Rogers?"

"Well, we always liked to. . . ." Suddenly her pleasant round face was turned away from us, and there were a few moments of embarrassed silence. Then she resumed. "We always gave Alan some little present when he had his leave. And this time we wanted it to be something special. I was going up to get it for him. I always say you can't get anything in the shops here."

"I see. But when you sent your telegram to Mr. Rogers, why didn't you say 'oo you was staying with? It wouldn't 'ave cost no more to've said, 'staying with Fairfaxes' than 'staying with friends.'"

Mrs. Rogers said in a quiet voice that made one think she would have smiled then if she could, " Well, to tell you the truth it was a sort of family joke with us that Mr. Rogers never cared for Mr. Fairfax. And I think Mrs. Fairfax knew that, because she suggested not mentioning names. She said that if Mr. Rogers knew he might go round to see Mr. Fairfax about it, and that wouldn't do."

" Well, thank you, Mrs. Rogers. That settles your part of yesterday." He sucked his moustache. " 'Oo's nephew was 'e by rights, yours or Mr. Rogers's?"

The old lady glanced at her husband. " Well, he wasn't either of our nephews, exactly," she said. " Sort of adopted nephew."

" No relation at all?"

" No. Not to say relation."

" 'Ow long ago did you take 'im on?"

" About seven years ago. You tell them, Alf."

She turned to the fire again, and her husband cleared his throat.

" There's not really much to tell," he said. " He came to my shop one day when we was in Bromley, and asked for work. Mother was out at the time, and I gave him something to eat, and he stayed talking. He was in a bad way—down and out. I took rather a fancy to the lad. We've never had any children of our own, you see. And when mother came home she liked him, too. So he stayed on for a day or two. And one thing led to another, and he's stayed with us ever since. But of course he was always anxious to get work. And after a bit he went back to his old line—steward on the ships."

"What was his real name, then?"

"We never knew. And as he didn't like talking about his past before he came to us, we never pressed him to find out. All he told us was that he'd been a steward before, and got into some trouble. He was a lad for trouble, you see, but nothing serious."

Beef's pencil scratched painfully on.

"Now this time 'ome," he said at last, "he didn't be'ave unusual?"

"No. Not that we noticed."

"Did he receive any letters?"

"One. From a girl, he said. Oh, and he did say when he saw the envelope that he thought he'd done with that."

"It was waiting for 'im when 'e got 'ome?"

"Yes."

"No others?"

"No. Not that we saw."

"'E didn't say anything unusual?"

"No. He was on about his young lady. He was engaged to Molly Cutler, you know."

"Yes, I know. 'E never said nothink about being followed?"

"Followed?" said Mr. Rogers. "No. Nothing at all."

"And about this walking out with Miss Cutler. You approved, did you?"

Mrs. Rogers answered at once. "Of course we did. A really nice young lady. We were very pleased. Why, his uncle wanted him to get married at once, didn't you, Alf? Mr. Rogers said if he liked to get married and not go back to sea, he'd help him set up in business. But he wouldn't hear of it. He said he had had quite enough from us. He wanted to save enough money on his own. He got good money at sea."

"You advised 'im to throw it up then, Mr. Rogers?"

"Well, I thought it was time he settled down."

"I see. Well, what did 'e do 'is first day 'ome?"

"He was messing about with his motor-bike most of the day. He nearly always takes it half to pieces every time he comes."

"Did 'e see anyone?"

"He went out in the evening—to meet his young lady."

"No one else?"

"Not that we know of."

"And yesterday?"

"He was gone from here at ten o'clock on his bike."

"Say where 'e was going?"

"No. 'E never mentioned anything like that. He did not like it if we asked him too many questions about his movements. That was his way."

"I see. When did you see him again?"

"Well, I've told you all that. Do you want me to go over it again in front of mother?"

Sergeant Beef turned back several pages of his notebook. "No. I don't think that's necessary.

I see I've got your information about his return.
It was about eight o'clock, you said?"

"Somewhere about then."

"What time do you shut the shop?"

"Between six and half-past."

"Same yesterday?"

"Yes."

"And you stayed in after that?"

"Oh no. I always have my walk after I've
shut up. I go up as far as the Memorial every
night."

"I see. What time do you get back, then?"

"It depends. Soon after seven, usually."

"Had your nephew got a key?"

"Yes."

"So that it would have been possible for 'im
to've come in and gone out again while you
was 'aving your walk?"

"I suppose it would. I never thought of
that."

"When 'e come in at eight o'clock, was 'e
on 'is motor-bike?"

"I really can't remember. I didn't notice.
To tell you the truth I was having forty winks
when he came in."

"You said last night he was wearing his
motor-biking things, though?"

"Yes. That's right."

"Oh. You never *eard* the bike?"

"Not as far as I can remember."

"'Ow did you first know it was back in the
shed in your yard, then?"

"The constable went to look, when he came
round last night."

"Thank you, Mr. Rogers. And now I should like to 'ave a look at 'is things."

Mrs. Rogers rose wearily to her feet. "I'll take you up," she said.

"No, mother, you stay by the fire," said her husband. "I'll go upstairs with the Sergeant."

But she shook her head. "I shouldn't like anyone to be touching Alan's things unless I were there," she said, and began to lead the way.

The dead man's bedroom was at the back of the little house, over the room in which we had been sitting. It was cold and rather cheerless this February afternoon, and had the slightly stuffy air of most cottage bedrooms. There was an iron bedstead, a dressing-table with another photo of Molly Cutler on it, and a trunk. Beef eyed the latter.

"'Fraid I shall 'ave to 'ave a look," he said, and opened the lid.

Young Rogers's belongings were so ordinary that they were soon examined. Suits, shirts, oddments of clothing, an electric torch, a camera, shoes, writing materials (but no letters), hairbrushes, and his steward's uniform.

"'E didn't seem to bring 'ome much from abroad," Beef reflected.

"Well, there was the Customs," said Mrs. Rogers.

"He never seemed to think it worth while," said her husband. "He said things were dearer out there than what they are here."

"I daresay," said Beef. "It's often the way."

He paused for a final look round the room

and noticed, hanging near the door, a suit of overalls. They were dark blue in colour, and seemed to be almost new. There was not a sign of dirt or grease on them anywhere.

"Nice clean overalls," Sergeant Beef reflected.

"Yes," said Mrs. Rogers. "He never used them, you' see. His uncle bought them for him over at Claydown a week or so back, didn't you, Dad? But he was silly about them, and bought them too small. We were laughing about them when Alan first got home. He was going to wear them to do his bike, but he couldn't get them on."

Beef fingered them for a minute. "Oh," he said.

Slowly we all went downstairs.

"I think that's all I need ask you for the moment," he said, "I'm sorry to 'ave 'ad to do it when you was both upset. But these things 'ave to be done. I'm sure if you think of anything else that might be useful you'll let me know."

"We'd like it all to be sifted out, Sergeant," said Mrs. Rogers. But it was plain that she was anxious for us to leave her alone, and I was relieved when I saw Beef making for the street. This had been the most trying half-hour I had faced with him.

CHAPTER VII

In the High Street a boy was selling evening papers. He had only two of the three which reached this town, but I purchased these. A glance at the front page was sufficient to show me that the case was going to be a much-advertised one.

Who was it that invented that ancient tag, supposed to be the Editor's advice to the new reporter? Dog bites man—not news. Man bites dog—news. Here was a case of it. These papers, tired, no doubt, of cases in which the task of the police was to find out who had killed So-and-So, were enjoying themselves with this strange reversal of the common case. Coming straight from the tragic household of the Rogers, I found their facetiousness in rather bad taste.

PUZZLE—FIND THE MURDER

was one heading, in the heavy type reserved for major sensations, and

MURDER—BUT NO CORPSE

was another.

Beef, glancing at these over my shoulder, snorted with disgust. Perhaps he too felt, after our visit to the Rogers', that there wasn't much room for humour in the case. But he did not pause as we took our way to the police station.

Here a surprise awaited him. The young constable whom I had met last night handed him a telegram. While Beef was reading it I glanced at the two men who were under his authority, and thought I discerned an exchange of smiles which seemed to say that they tolerated the Sergeant amiably. It certainly took Beef a long time to study the telegram, but I hoped that these smarter, and probably better-educated young men, were not smirking at his slowness. However, I made no remark.

"They're coming down," said Beef at last.

"Who, Sergeant, the Yard?" asked one of the constables.

"Detective-Inspector Stute," said Beef.

"Good Lord! He's the big noise just now. They must think a lot of this case. It's all the newspaper publicity, I suppose."

Beef turned to me. "It's a funny thing," he said, "they wouldn't 'ear of it when I arst them this morning. I was all at sea then. And now, just as I begin to get a bit of an idea of the case, down they come. Oh, well. They'll soon puzzle it out."

"Think they will?" I asked. My knowledge of Scotland Yard has been gained from detective novels, and was not flattering to the Force.

"'Course they will. This 'ere Stute's a wonder. 'E gets at the truf of anythink before you can say knife. They 'ave all the latest methods, too. I shan't be able to do nothink now, except show 'em round. It's a pity—just when I was beginning to sort it out."

I realized, very plainly, the truth of what my

old friend Beef had said. Hitherto his slow if certain wits had only been in competition with the amateur detectives, in a case which Scotland Yard had not thought worth investigating. This time he would be confronted with the keen and practised intelligence of the professional. Glancing at his red and rustic face, I realized that he could not hope to do more than show the big man about, as he suggested, and perhaps here and there put in a word, the result of his muddled cogitations, which would help. I felt that in contrast to Detective-Inspector Stute, whose name I had already heard, Sergeant Beef would present a figure that would justify the smiles of his two young constables. However, having nothing to do for a few days, I decided to stay on, and see how he progressed.

"There's one more call I'd like to make," said Sergeant Beef to me, when we had left the station, "before the Detective gets down. That's the Riverside Private Hotel, where this Mist'r an' Misses Fairfax was staying."

"Very well," I said, and we set off together.

Braxham is built beside the River Jade, and at one time must have relied on the water as a means of transport. Near the railway station there are a number of old warehouses, some of them empty, the foundations of which are lapped by the water, while between them are cuts running to the river's edge. We had to pass these on our way out to the Riverside Private Hotel, which was also on the river, but with lawns running down to a landing-stage. Beyond the warehouses, beyond the station, we went, into a more pretentious district where large, red-brick houses had been built during the last seventy years.

In the summer, one felt, this region would be pleasant, with its flowering trees and gardens, and beneath it the river, or even an occasional small yacht. But on this February evening it was damp and cheerless.

Riverside Private Hotel turned out to consist of one of the largest of these houses, a pseudo-gothic affair in dull red brick, built towards the beginning of this century. There was a long drive running between dripping laurel bushes, and a flight of steps up to the front door. Beef explained his business to a neat servant, and we were shown into a small room which was furnished rather like an office, and told that Mrs. Murdoch would be with us in a moment.

When she appeared, I thought her rather formidable. She was tall, raw-boned, severe, and almost certainly of Scotch origin. She looked at Beef disapprovingly, but told us to sit down, and appeared to be resigned to the necessity of giving us what information she could.

"Oo's these Fairfaxes?" began Beef abruptly.

"Mr. and Mrs. Fairfax are clients of mine of two years' standing."

"*What* are they, though?"

"I beg your pardon?"

"I mean, wot's 'e do for a living?"

"I really couldn't say. His profession is no possible concern of mine."

"Doesn't 'e fill in the usual form then?" asked Beef aggressively.

Mrs. Murdoch rose with dignity to her feet, and pulled an ornamental bell-cord. On the appearance of the maid who had opened the door to us, she said, "The Visitors' Book, Wilkins."

Beef decided to be pleasant. "That's right," he said, "I thought you must 'ave some record."

But Mr. Fairfax's record, when found, said only that he was British, coming from London, and by profession "Company Promoter," a vague term.

"Is 'e still 'ere?" asked Beef.

"No. Weren't you aware that he left yesterday?"

"Yesterday? Wot time?"

"He left the hotel with young Rogers at approximately two o'clock."

"With young Rogers? 'Ere, this sounds interesting. Wot was 'e doing with young Rogers?"

"They had lunched together, here."

"Wot about 'is wife?"

"She had left for London that morning."

"So she 'ad. I'd forgotten that. So young Rogers was 'ere yesterday. Wot time did 'e get 'ere?"

"At one o'clock or so. Not later. Mr. Fairfax probably stressed the necessity for punctuality in this house."

"Did 'e come on his motor-bike?"

"I believe so. There was a lot of noise in the drive."

"You didn't see, then?"

"No. The motor-bicycle, if it was a motor-bicycle, was left round the bend of the drive."

"You 'ad a look then, did you?" Beef sounded almost roguish.

Mrs. Murdoch spoke loftily. "I glanced from a window to see what all the noise was. I saw young Rogers walking up, having left his motor-bike near the gate. Once before I had asked him not to make a fiendish noise under the windows with it. We have elderly persons and invalids here, who like to sleep during the afternoon."

"Then 'e came in and 'ad 'is dinner with this 'ere Fairfax?"

"Lunch, yes."

"And when did 'e go?"

"Mr. Fairfax accompanied him at about 2 o'clock."

"Did 'e take 'is bike then?"

"No. Not then. He came for it, I believe, about three-quarters of an hour later."

"You 'eard 'im start it up?"

"One couldn't help it."

"And Fairfax?"

"Mr. Fairfax has not returned."

"Well, I'm blowed. Wot about 'is luggage?"

"It remains in his room. Quite untouched, of course."

"That's funny."

"I beg your pardon?"

"I mean it's funny 'is not showing up again."

"I thought it somewhat curious myself. And, of course, his account is unpaid."

"Come 'ere often did 'e?"

"About every two months or so."

"Whatever for?"

Mrs. Murdoch squared her shoulders. "Most

of my clients repeat their visits. And there was the fishing."

"I know. But it's only a bit of coarse fishing. Perch, and roach and that."

"Still, Mr. Fairfax was very fond of it."

"And 'e gave no 'int that 'e might be leaving yesterday?"

"On the contrary, I had understood that he required his room for three or four days at least."

"Wot about 'is wife? Did she know?"

"I think not. She has gone back to town expecting him after the week-end."

"She was fed up wiv it down 'ere, I suppose?"

Mrs. Murdoch answered with dignity. "Mrs. Fairfax did not fish," she said.

Sergeant Beef looked up from his notebook. "And there isn't nothink else as you could tell me?"

Mrs. Murdoch coughed. "I have Mr. Fairfax's London address," she said.

"That might come in useful," said Beef. "I'll note it down." And with great care he did so.

That appeared to be all the information that Beef wanted or could get from Mrs. Murdoch.

"I tell you wot though," he said, "I should like a word wiv the girl wot giv' 'em their dinner yesterday. She might 'ave 'eard somethink."

"The *waiter* who served Mr. Fairfax at lunch yesterday can come and speak to you," said Mrs. Murdoch. "But the servants are not encouraged to listen to private conversation among the guests. And now I will ask you to excuse me. I trust that the name of the Riverside

Private Hotel will be used as little as possible in connection with this unpleasant case."

The way in which she enunciated the word "unpleasant" suggested that Beef himself was involved in the general nausea of the business.

"That's not for me to say, Ma'am. You better get on to the newspapers about that. They'd say anythink."

Mrs. Murdoch rose. "It's all very unsavoury," she said. "I'll send the waiter to you. Good evening." She marched from the room resolutely.

Beef blew violently through his lips, so that his moustache wavered outwards. "'Ow 'ud you like to work for 'er?" he whispered. "An' she never suggested us 'aving a drop of nothink, either. Still that's interesting wot she said about young Rogers being 'ere with that Fairfax, isn't it?"

The waiter, an elderly man correctly dressed, came in.

"Did you give Mr. Fairfax 'is . . . lunch yesterday?" asked Beef.

"Yes. I served the gentlemen."

"Didn't 'ear nothink did you?"

"I don't quite understand," said the waiter haughtily.

"All right, my lad," said Beef. "The old girl's not 'ere now. You needn't be up in the air. Wot was they talking about?"

"I never listen. . . ."

"Come off of it. Come off of it. Wot did they say?"

"I did happen to gather that the gist of their talk referred to the younger gentleman's occupation. Mr. Fairfax was emphatic in his advice to him to leave the sea, and settle down ashore."

"Is that all?"

"That is all I heard."

"Was they talking secret at all?"

"Oh no. Quite openly."

"Didn't say nothink about that afternoon?"

"I heard nothing beyond what I've told you."

"All right. That'll do."

Out in the damp evening, Beef pondered. "Funny, 'is not 'aving told 'is uncle and aunt 'e was going to 'ave dinner wiv Fairfax."

"Unless it was because old Rogers didn't like Fairfax, you remember what Mrs. Rogers said."

"Yes. So she did," said Beef.

c

CHAPTER VIII

I was determined not to be left out of the case now, even if Detective-Inspector Stute was going to take it up. So that next morning I went round to the police station, asked for the Sergeant, and was shewn in to the office in which he and Stute were already in conference.

There was, of course, no reason why I should be admitted, but my reading of detective novels, which had been considerable, had taught me that an outsider, with no particular excuse, was often welcomed on these occasions, especially if he had the gift of native fatuity, and could ask ludicrous questions at the right moment, so I hoped for the best. Beef introduced me without explanation, Stute nodded amicably and indicated a chair, and I was at home. That, I thought, is one good thing that writers of detective novels have done—taught Scotland Yard to admit miscellaneous strangers to their most secret conclaves.

Stute was a well-dressed man in his fifties, with thick grey hair, a young man's complexion, and a neat military moustache. He might have been, and probably was, an ex-officer. He might have been, but probably wasn't, a graduate of Oxford or Cambridge. He was listening to Beef with close attention, and the Sergeant was evidently finishing his recital.

"So that's as far's I've got, sir," he said. "I'm very glad you've come. Course, you'll soon clear it all up, but I could see from the beginning it was too much for me."

"It didn't sound too much, Sergeant," said Stute. "We thought the body would turn up at once. But there you are. We must get down to it."

He leant back in his chair, offered us cigarettes, drew slowly at one himself, then said, "It seems pretty certain that the murder was committed between 2.15 when Fairfax and Young Rogers left the Mitre and 8.0 when he reached his home."

Beef said nothing. He evidently thought his best policy was to leave all speculation and summary to Stute.

"Then again, so far as the information you have brought to light goes, there are three possibilities in the matter of who has been murdered—Fairfax, the girl Smythe, and the foreigner who came into the Mitre, unless, of course, this foreigner is to be identified with the one Mr. Townsend saw later. Probably as soon as we start making enquiries, we shall find two of them alive and well, and have a pretty good idea that it was the third. Get me the Yard on the 'phone, and I'll have the Fairfaxes traced right away. We shall have to get a little more information about the other two first."

Beef went to the door. "Galsworthy . . ." he began.

"What did you say?" asked Stute.

"I was speaking to the constable, sir."

"You don't mean to say you have a constable called Galsworthy, Sergeant?"

"Yes, sir."

"My God! All right. Go on."

"Galsworthy," said the Sergeant again, as though there had been no interruption, "get Scotland Yard on the 'phone."

"What we want here," said Stute, when Beef was sitting before him again, "is system. First, the dead man. Had the bloodstains examined?"

"No, sir."

"Contents of the bottle analysed?"

"No, sir."

"Really, Sergeant. Those should have been your first steps."

The buzzer warned him to lift up the receiver beside him, and in a few moments he was reading out the address of Mr. and Mrs. Fairfax in Hammersmith, and enjoining whoever attended to it to ring him up as soon as the information was through. I liked his brisk and businesslike method of attack.

"Now that coat," he said, "and the shirt."

Beef pulled them out of a cupboard, and handed them to him. Stute examined them carefully.

"Yes," he said, "I should say that was blood. Send them off to the research department. And the bottle to the analyst."

"Galsworthy!" I could see Stute shudder. "Pack these up. Send the coat and shirt for research, and the bottle for analysis. See?"

Galsworthy repressed a smile, I thought, as he said, "Very well, Sergeant."

"What about his boots? Examined those?"

"I did 'ave a look at 'em."

"Let me see them," sighed Stute. "What's the soil round here?"

"Very poor, sir. My scarlet runners last year. . . ."

"Never mind your scarlet runners, Beef. What is it? Loam? Clay? What?"

"Nasty chalky sort of soil, sir."

"Same everywhere about?"

"Yessir."

Stute had turned the boots over carefully, scraped a little at the sole, and put them down. He picked up each piece of the dead man's clothing in turn and examined it carefully but without remark. Next he demanded to see the black motor-cycling oilskins that Rogers had worn earlier in the day, and Beef had to send for them, swiftly and surreptitiously, from Rogers's shop.

"What we've got to do," he said, "is first of all to follow as much as we can of young Rogers's movements on the day of the murder. And by that time we may be able to eliminate one or more of the candidates for the rôle of murderee. We know he left his home at 10.30. Where did he go?"

"That I can't say, sir."

"Well then, come along, we'll take the car, and see what we can find. Soon straighten this up, Beef. Only you need System, Method, Efficiency. Off we go." And he jumped to his feet and led the way to his police car at the door.

Poor old Beef! I couldn't help considering

once again that his solution of the Thurston mystery must have been the merest luck. He looked such a floundering old fellow beside this brisk detective. But I did not like to hear him reprimanded quite so brusquely. After all, he had never pretended to be anything but a country policeman, and he had done his best.

We went to the little bootmaking establishment kept by the Rogers. Mrs. Rogers joined her husband behind the counter. She was calmer to-day, but still looked tired and unhappy. No. They were quite sure he hadn't mentioned where he was going. No, they had no idea that he was lunching with Mr. Fairfax. Why wouldn't he have told them?

"Well," explained Mrs. Rogers, "father never cared much for the Fairfaxes, as I told you. And Alan may have thought he wouldn't have liked it if he had known he was going to see Mr. Fairfax."

"What had you against them?" Stute asked old Rogers.

"Nothing, really. There was a bit of swank with them, I always thought."

"Did you know when he was meeting Miss Cutler?"

"Yes. He had told us that. Seven o'clock."

"And you've no idea where he could have gone between the two?"

"No. None. I only wish we had."

Beef drew Mrs. Rogers aside to tell her the date and time of the inquest, and this seemed to upset her again, for we left her on the verge of tears.

"They seemed to have been very fond of this fellow," remarked Stute as we entered the car.

"But '*e* was no good," said Beef.

"He has succeeded in bewildering the police, anyway," replied Stute rather uncharitably. "I think, before we go any further, I should like a little more information about his past."

When we had returned to the station, Stute told Beef that if he would put the telephone through to the exchange, he would get Scotland Yard himself. It seemed that he had no wish to hear a repetition of the constable's elaborate and literary name, pronounced by Sergeant Beef. I sat back and listened, greatly impressed, while he gave his curt but thorough instructions. Young Rogers's fellow stewards were to be examined. His friends on board were to be identified and questioned. The Chief Steward was to be asked for information, and the Purser. Then, I heard, the Buenos Aires police were to be asked if they knew anything of young Rogers's record while he had been in that country.

Stute put his hand over the mouthpiece, and turned to Beef. "Taken his finger-prints?" he asked.

"'Oo's?" said Beef.

"Good heavens, man. Young Rogers's of course."

"No, I 'aven't."

"Then do so at once." He turned again to the telephone. "I'll send you two sets of finger-prints to-morrow. Send one of them to Buenos Aires and get them to look them up."

Sergeant Beef seemed to be pondering something, as Stute finished speaking.

"Well, Beef?"

"I was just wondering, sir, what use it was
sending them finger-prints out to . . . where-
ever you said they was to go."

"What use? What do you mean?"

"I mean, wot could they do wiv' 'em? They
don't know wot to look 'im up under. They
'aven't even got 'is right name!"

There was a suggestion of triumph in Beef's
voice. Indeed it did look as though he had
caught the detective out in a blunder.

But Stute, instead of being annoyed, smiled.
He leaned back, lit another cigarette, and
turned to Beef.

"It's just the sort of thing you have to know
when you get to the Yard, Sergeant." His quiet
cultured voice sounded complacent. "Though
of course none of us can know everything."

"Wot is?" asked Beef, still evidently under
the impression that the other had tripped up.

"This. The Argentine Police have a very
efficient system of finger-print cataloguing—
quite different from any other. In fact, in the
International Police Conference of New York
a few years ago they surprised us all. It is called
the Vucetich System, because it was invented
by a man called Juan Vucetich thirty years
ago."

"Go on!" The exclamation was one of deep
interest, rather than an invitation to proceed.

"Instead of classifying their finger-prints under
names, nature of crimes, district, or by any of

the methods used by other countries, they classify them according to certain fundamental types of finger-print. This has obvious advantages. Given a complete and clear set of finger-prints they can trace, among their enormous archives, the man to whom they belong."

"Well, I'm blowed!" exclaimed Beef, very much impressed.

"Everyone in the country, whether Argentine or not, has his prints taken when he needs an identification card, and they've got millions of 'em. Here, as you know, we only take them when a man is charged. Of course, it doesn't always work. But in 1934 their records show that out of 513 sets of prints handed them for identification in criminal cases, they had been able to put their hand on the owners of 327 of them. Which is very good indeed."

"I should think it was!" said Beef, rather agape. "But, 'ow can they classify 'em, sir?"

"There are four fundamental types of print," pronounced the detective, "as you could see by sufficient study. These are distinguishable by the way in which the lines are formed in the finger-print itself. But . . . we're wasting time, Sergeant. I can't stop to give you a lecture on finger-prints."

"And you mean to say that by sending young Rogers's prints out to . . . that place you was mentioning, we may be able to find out wot 'is real name was?"

"It's more than likely."

"Well, I dunno," said Beef. "Seems to me it's no good trying. You've got all these 'ere modern methods wot we knows nothink about."

Stute smiled kindly. "Never mind, Beef. You can only keep at it. There's a lot of luck in the game, remember."

"Thank you, sir," said Beef, and seemed delighted when the detective decided to knock off for an hour while we all had lunch.

CHAPTER IX

BEEF had asked me back to his house for what he modestly called a "bit of dinner," and we found his wife waiting for us in the kitchen living room. She was a chirpy little woman with sharp but pleasant features, hair tightly screwed, and gold-rimmed glasses.

"It's all ready," she said when introductions were over, and we sat down round a scrupulously clean table-cloth.

"And do you share your husband's interest in crime?" I asked.

"Gracious no. I leave all that to Beef. I never like hearing about such things. I won't even read about them in the papers. Help yourself to Brussels, won't you?"

"But surely . . ." I began.

"No, it's no good. Nasty creepy murders. Not but what they tell me Beef's clever at putting his hand on the one who's done it. But I always say leave that to those that like it. It's not for me to poke my nose in. Oh, and while I think of it, Beef, that Mr. Sawyer was round this morning."

"Wot Mr. Sawyer?" asked Beef, his mouth too full.

"Why from the Dragon. He said he wanted to see you urgent."

"That means 'e's fixed another darts match," said Beef, evidently delighted.

"No. It was something to do with young Rogers, he said."

Beef turned to me. "Orways get a lot of that," he said, "people as wants to think they knows somethink. Still, I suppose we shall 'ave to see 'im. Why did 'e come 'ere instead of the station?"

"Now how am I to know?" said Mrs. Beef. "Hand this gentleman some more parsnips and help yourself."

"It's funny, that," said Beef. "The Dragon's that pub down by the station. I don't use it a great deal. I'd sooner 'ave the Mitre. The beer's better, and the darts board's lit prop'ly. 'Owever, we can pop in there later on."

"And don't stay all night," said Mrs. Beef. "There's a good wireless programme coming on at ten o'clock, and it would be a pity to miss it."

"You ought to know by now," said Beef quite amiably, "that when I've got an important case on, there's no telling *what* time I shall be 'ome."

"Well, there never is, as far as I can see. Case or no case. But still. Have some treacle roll, will you, Mr. Townsend?"

There was plainly an excellent understanding between them—Mrs. Beef being tolerant of her husband's weaknesses, while having a certain respect for his success, and Beef appreciating his wife's good humour and cooking. When I had bade good-bye and thanked her and been told to come again "whenever I was passing," we set out for the station again, feeling warmed and filled.

Stute was waiting impatiently. "Good heavens, Beef," he said, "does it take you all day to eat? I had a sandwich and was back here half an hour ago. I'd like to see how some of you fellows would get on in London, with a really big case keeping everyone on his toes."

"Sorry, sir," grumbled Beef.

"There's some important news here. My man has been round to the flat occupied by Fairfax and his wife. The wife left yesterday morning, and Fairfax, apparently, has never returned there. No one was in the flat at all last night, and when Mrs. Fairfax left she took two suit-cases. What do you think of that?"

"That's funny," said Beef.

"Funny? I wish I shared your sense of the comic. It complicates things immensely."

Beef cleared his throat. "I 'ave something to report also," he said.

"Well?"

"That is—I shall 'ave. Mr. Sawyer, 'oo keeps the Dragon 'Otel near the station, 'as some information for me connected with this 'ere turn-out wot 'e says is urgent."

"Indeed? Perhaps he has discovered the corpse in one of his beer barrels."

"Well, for all you could taste the difference in 'is beer 'e might of," said Beef. "It's the most poisonous. . . ."

"If you would give a little less attention to beer, and a little more to the matter we are investigating, Beef, we should get on more quickly. I've sent your men round the town to see whether they can pick up any information from the local gossips. Though how you expect people to respect a policeman with a name like Galsworthy, I don't know. Now come along. We'll call in at this pub and see your man then go out to Chopley and see what we can find out about this other girl. We've got to get our information tabulated."

"Yessir."

The Dragon proved to be a dreary looking public house in a rather grimy street which ran parallel to the river and towards the station. It stood among the warehouses we had noticed yesterday, and its back premises must have gone down to the water's edge. It was narrow and tall, its boards painted green and its paint-work dirty. The lace curtains across its upper windows were limp and grey and its aspect was altogether uninviting. It was the sort of house which, built in a working class area, sold immense quantities of liquor, and troubled little about its amenities.

We had arrived after hours, so that Beef had to hammer for a long time on the side-door before it was opened. But at last an immensely stout man appeared. His face was bloated and crimson, and the grotesque enormity of his stomach was accentuated by the fact that he wore no jacket.

"Nice time to come," he said. "I was just going to have my dinner."

"I'm sorry, Mr. Sawyer," said Beef. "I only just got your message."

Stute was impatient, and when the publican

stood aside he hurried in by the small space left between abdomen and wall.

"Now then," he said brusquely, "what have you to tell us?"

"This gent's from Scotland Yard," said Beef aside to Sawyer.

The publican was disgruntled. He had pictured the giving of his information as a leisurely and enjoyable affair over a glass of bitter. It was unpleasant to have his importance as one possessing special knowledge exploded by this curt stranger.

"It's not much," he said sulkily. "Only he came in here that evening."

"'Oo? Rogers?"

"Yes."

"What time?" snapped Stute.

"Well," said the publican sarcastically, "not knowing that he had just done someone in, or was just going to do someone in, I never made a special note of the time. But I can tell you it wasn't many minutes after I'd opened at six o'clock."

"Say 6.10?" Stute asked.

"Round about then."

"And? What did he say?"

"What did he say? He said a double Scotch and a splash, if you want to know."

"Nothing else?"

"Nothing much. He mentioned he'd just seen someone off on the six o'clock train."

"Oh, he mentioned that. Did he say who it was?"

"No."

"Did he look normal?"

"Normal?"

"Did he look himself, I mean? Anything unusual about him?"

"He was quiet. Very quiet."

"Nothing else?"

"No."

"Do you know if he came on his motor-bike?"

"Yes. I heard him start it up afterwards."

"Where did he leave it?"

"Well, I haven't got a proper parking place. And rather than leave it in the road, I suppose, he put it down the alley beside the house."

"Where does that lead to?"

"Down to the river."

"I see. What was he wearing?"

"He had on all his motor-biking kit. Black oilskin stuff and a cap over his ears."

"Thanks Mr. Sawyer. Come along, Sergeant. We haven't time to waste."

And with a curt nod to the publican Detective Stute made for the door at his businesslike pace. I could just hear some mumbled swearing from Mr. Sawyer, or Beef, or both, behind me.

Out in the open air, Stute was already examining the alley. It was narrow, and its ground was of darkish muddy cinders. One side of it was formed by the public house, the other by an empty warehouse, which rose to a considerable height of blank wall. We picked our way among the puddles to the water's edge.

Stute was looking up at the wall of the Dragon, in which there was only one window, and that on the first floor. But when he turned his attention to the warehouse, he gave a sudden sound which came as near to excitement as Stute would allow himself to go. For along the front of the warehouse, above the river itself, was a long wooden platform, built out over the water, to enable boats to be unloaded. And down to the alley from this were some rough steps.

We were soon on the platform, and Stute was going over the floor of it like a fox-hound. He looked down into the water, he looked along under the walls, he tried the two doors of the warehouse, so absorbed that he seemed to have forgotten Beef and me who stood rather sheepishly by.

"It's a possibility," he said at last. "Beef!"

"Yessir?"

"Tell your men to search every inch of this building, will you?"

"Yessir."

"Very well. Now we'll make for Chopley."

CHAPTER X

BETWEEN Braxham and Chopley was a heath.
You may call it a common, if you like, in fact
you would be correct in doing so. But viewed
on that February afternoon from the police car,
it seemed so barren and forbidding that I was
reminded of Macbeth and his three witches. It
was, after all, the possible, the very possible,
scene of a murder. Under one of the scrubby
gorse-bushes which we could see might even
now be lying the body of young Rogers's
victim.

It was not an enjoyable ride. Stute and Beef
remained for the most part silent, and I watched
the bleak miles go by, wondering why I spent
my time in this odd way, and wishing, I'm afraid,
that I was back in my comfortable London flat.

The distance was about ten miles, but we
passed through no intermediate village. There
were a few houses built near the road, and a
disused windmill away to our right, but for the
most part we kept away from humanity.

"'E could've done it out 'ere somewheres,"
observed Beef suddenly.

"Undoubtedly, Sergeant. But there are a
good many places in which he *could* have done it.
It is our job to be definite. Now very soon we
shall be able to follow most of his movements on
that day. It seems, in fact, that we have only

to visit sufficient licensed premises to complete it. We already know that he was in the Mitre at 2.15 and the Dragon at 6.10. I hope to-night we can draw up a time-table of his day. That will be a step forward. You see? Order. Method. You can't beat it."

The steeple of Chopley Church was before us now, and we all looked ahead. At the entrance to the village a constable stood beside his bicycle, and Stute drew the car up to him. The constable saluted.

"I was expecting you, sir. Mrs. Walker's who you want. Go right through the village, and bear to the left at the fork. You'll find her cottage about a hundred yards down on the right. Rose Cottage, it's called."

"Thank you. What's your name?"

"Smith, sir."

Stute nodded, and drove on. "I was afraid it might be Kipling or Stevenson," he said aside to Beef.

"'Ow did 'e know wot we was after?" Beef asked.

"There *is* such a thing as a telephone. And while you were taking your hour and five minutes for lunch, Sergeant, I made use of it. It has saved us time, you see, and time's everything. Here we are."

We had stopped at the gate of a small square cottage standing back from the road. There was a sign-board hanging in front of us on which the words "Teas. Refreshments. Accommodation for Cyclists," appeared, while on the gate was the name Rose Cottage.

I was growing a little tired of these interviews with publicans and landladies, carried out in the hope of completing what Stute called "a time-table" of young Rogers's movements. I had not the same passion for time-tables, lists, method and order, as Stute had. And when I saw Mrs. Walker, the woman we were about to question, I felt even less anxious for another of these contacts.

She was red-headed, middle-aged, and aggressive. Indeed she had come out of her cottage before we had reached the gate, and began to talk before even Stute could address her.

"So you've come at last," she said as she hurried down the path towards us, looking rather untidy and unkempt, "I've been waiting in for you all day, though I might have known that the police would leave this till last when they ought to have come here first. And when I think of that poor murdered girl. . . ."

"We should like to ask you several questions," said Stute frigidly.

"Yes. And there are some questions I should like to ask *you!*" said Mrs. Walker as she led the way into Rose Cottage. "Letting a girl get murdered and then not even knowing why or where, and not troubling to come here and find out. I call it nothing short of wicked. Why, anyone might have her throat cut in her bed, and you wouldn't trouble to lift a finger for two or three days, let alone find out who had done it. I could have told you from the start all about this if you had just come to see me, but there you are, everywhere but where you're wanted, it's always the way."

"I'm sure your evidence will be very valuable, Mrs. Walker. Now. . . ."

"Of course it will. Don't I know the whole circumstances from the time he brought her down here first, and told me they were married? I could see what he was then, the young black-guard, and that poor girl. . . ."

"How long ago would that have been?" asked Stute.

It seemed that both he and Beef had given up all hope of asking her formal questions, and were resigned now to allowing her talk to flow on, hoping to deflect it now and again into the channels which interested them.

"How long ago? I'm sure I couldn't say. Wait a minute, though. It was just after Christ-mas. It must have been two years ago. There was that heavy fall of snow if you remember, and they was fooling about with snow-balls in the front here. That gave them away if nothing else did. Who ever heard of a married couple snowballing one another. So I knew very well what it was, and what *he* was, too, the young scoundrel. But I held my tongue and waited, though I often heard of his goings-on from a lady friend of mine from Braxham who comes over now and again, and told me how he was took up by the Sergeant over there a couple of months ago for being drunk and disorderly and I don't know what else."

"But . . ."

"Wait a minute, can't you? I must have time to tell you what I know. *You've* waited long enough before coming to hear it, it won't hurt you to wait a few seconds longer while I get my breath. What was my surprise when a month ago I got a letter from that poor girl whose body's lying out on the common at this minute getting frozen while you're sitting here, asking me if I could tell her anything about that Rogers. She said I should remember who she was because she was the girl who'd come down with him before, which of course I did. The letter gave me a nasty turn, as you can imagine, to think it had happened here, and I wrote back telling her what I knew about him and that as I'd found out from my friend in Braxham he'd been home on leave again before long, and that he was nephew to the old Rogerses. So she wrote back and said she'd like to tackle him in person, and could I let her a room for a few days while he was home so that she could be on the spot which like a fool I said I could, little thinking I should be bringing the poor girl down to her death."

"Have you kept those letters of hers, Mrs. Walker?"

"No. Of course I haven't. Whatever should I want to keep letters for? There's enough litter in a place like this without letters. But what I was going to say was she came down and having written to young Rogers, she was waiting for him to come over. She said she'd got letters from him written when they was carrying on, saying he wanted to marry her, and she meant to make him behave decently by her, particularly when I told her what I'd heard from my friend in Braxham that he was carrying on with that Cutler girl. Well, on the Tuesday night she went to a dance at the village hall here with a commercial gentleman who was staying in the house and didn't get back till late. She'd told me earlier she was going and didn't want to be disturbed next day till twelve o'clock at the earliest, and if young Rogers came over I was to tell him so. And on the Wednesday sure enough he *did* come over in the morning. . . ."

"What time?" put in Stute, courageously.

"Time? I can't really say. It must have been round about eleven because the butcher's van was just about leaving as he came up on his motor-bike, and the butcher's very regular in his time. Well, this young Rogers speaks as though he's never seen me before, though of course he knew me from the time he'd brought the girl here before, and asks if she's in. So I told him she couldn't be disturbed before mid-day, and he got quite nasty about it, and said he hadn't got time to hang about here all the morning for *her*. So I told him to please himself and he didn't like that either, but he saw it was no good, so he said he'd got to lunch with some-one but he'd come back that afternoon, and if she wanted to see him she'd better be in, and off he goes on his motor-bike at a terrible speed, and I went up to tell Miss Smythe what he'd said."

"What impression had you of Miss Smythe?"

"Well, she was a bit stagey of course and all that, but you can't blame a girl for doing the best she can for herself nowadays, especially when it's a young fellow like this Rogers who'd treat anyone like dirt if he got the chance. He was back here at four o'clock and I gave them tea and left'them to it. What was my surprise an hour later. . . ."

"In the meantime you had heard nothing of what had passed between'them?"

"Certainly not. I never listen to other people's conversation, besides the wall between the tea-room and the kitchen is too thick to hear any-thing and whenever I went into the room they shut up like deckchairs and waited till I'd shut the door before they went on with what they were saying. But after an hour or so, Miss Smythe comes out to me and says everything's settled and she's going back to London. It wasn't my business and I hoped she'd arranged matters satisfactory, but I only said very well, and that I'd get her bill out for her, which I did and she paid it at once when she'd come down from packing her bag."

"What sort of bag?"

"Oh, she only had a sort of attach case with her, which didn't take her long to put together, and there she was ready to go. I asked her what train she was going to catch, and she said that young Rogers was going to take her into Braxham to get the six o'clock that being the fast. I said she seemed in a hurry to get back to London, and she said she was. She wasn't used to the country, she said, and didn't care much for it, which is small wonder when you come to think of it, because it couldn't be much quieter than what it is down here. . . ."

"So they went off together? What was she wearing?"

"She had on a sort of white mackintosh affair, rather smart. She was sitting behind him holding on round his waist. He was all dressed up in a black oilskin such as they use for motor-cycling. She was sitting on her attaché case which she said didn't matter because it was an old one, and as it's turned out of course it didn't, poor girl, nor did anything else once that fellow had got her out on the Common and gone for her. . . ."

"But what makes you so certain, Mrs. Walker, that he killed her?"

"Certain? Well, what else can anyone think? I read in the papers how he confessed to killing someone, and she's never been seen again, has she? Besides, he had his reasons, when the girl was trying to get her due. Of course he killed her, and if you'd only take the trouble you'd find her body out there somewhere at this minute."

"Perhaps you'd be surprised to hear, Mrs. Walker, that there are at least two other persons unaccounted for, either of whom may be the one murdered?"

For a moment I thought that Mrs. Walker at last was flummoxed. But she was equal to it.

"Oh no," she said, "I shouldn't be surprised. Not if there were a dozen, I shouldn't. That fellow was capable of murdering all three of them you mention, and I shouldn't be at all surprised if he hadn't done it!"

That was certainly a new and startling point of view.

CHAPTER XI

"Gor," said Beef, when we were at last in the car. "She didn't 'arf run on, did she? I wonder you never stopped 'er, sir."

"You've a lot to learn, Sergeant," returned Stute. "There are times when it is better to let people talk than to make them talk. Mrs. Walker's story had a certain amount of waste in it, but we got the information we wanted."

I thought that the man's description of Mrs. Walker's irrelevances as "waste" was typical of him. There was no "waste" from Stute; he went from point to point with dour economy.

"She has enabled us at least to fill in a little more of the time-table. The only important gaps now are the times between 11 o'clock and 1, between 2.15 and 4, and between 6.30 and 8.15."

"Yessir," said Beef with resignation.

As we were leaving the village, the young constable who had told us the position of Rose Cottage put out his hand to indicate that he wished to speak to Stute. He hurried across to the car, and Stute dropped the window beside his seat.

"Yes, Smith?"

"There's something more I thought you ought to know. At about 5.10 on that day, this young Rogers, with the girl who had been staying at

Rose Cottage, went into the village general
store."

"Well?"

"He left his motorbike outside, and the two
of them entered together. He asked if they sold
rope."

"Rope?" asked Stute quickly, and I thought
there was a flash of special interest in his glance.

"Yes, sir. Mrs. Davies said she'd only got the
complete clothes-lines, which are done up in
skeins of twelve yards, and the young lady asked
if she couldn't sell them a smaller quantity as
they only wanted it to fasten an attaché case on
the motor-bicycle. Mrs. Davies said she couldn't
cut them, and the man said he'd take the whole
thing."

"Did she watch them tie it on?"

"I asked her that, sir, and she said that the
shop was full and she didn't notice, but she
thinks it was some minutes before the motor-bike
started up outside. That was all she knew, sir."

"Thank you, Smith. Very useful," said Stute,
and began driving on. "I wonder," he said to
Beef, "whether a man with a name like Thack-
eray, or whatever it was, would have got that
information for me?"

Beef was piqued. "I wonder," he said, and
then was silent. I rather sympathised with him.
There was something almost priggish about
Smith.

We were speeding over the Common again,
and I could not help thinking of Mrs. Walker's
gruesome conviction that Stella Smythe's body
was even now lying on this waste land. It

seemed that the same thought had come to Stute, for he spoke to Beef without taking his eyes from the road ahead.

"We shall have to have this place searched," he said.

"Very good, sir," said Beef, still rather sulky.

The rest of the drive was passed with little conversation, and I sat at the back of the car wondering what conclusions were being reached in the minds of the two investigators.

At the police station Stute was told that a man was waiting to see him, and when we had sat down once again in Beef's little office, he was ushered in. His name, it appears, was Charles Meadows, and he was a porter employed at the railway station.

"Evening, Sarge," he said with somewhat too much familiarity.

Beef cleared his throat. "Good evening, Meadows," he returned in his most solemn voice. "Wot can I do for you?"

Mr. Meadows, who was a pale and rather peaked little man in his forties, leaned forward with an air of having a secret to confide. "I've got something to tell you," he said.

Stute broke in. "We're very busy," he said. "What is it you want to say?"

Mr. Meadows looked hurt. "I was trying to help," he said.

"Well, well. What can you tell us?"

"I saw young Rogers that evening when I was coming off duty," he said.

"What time was that?"

"About ten to six, it would have been."

"Where?"

"Well, I live out on the Chopley Road. I was walking along, not thinking of anything in particular, till I got past the last house in the avenue, and was going along that bit where the road goes across to our cottages. . . ."

"That's not very explicit," Stute cut in. "Do you mean that there is a stretch of road without any houses on it between the last outskirts of this town and the place where you live?"

"That's right, sir." Poor Mr. Meadows was quite subdued by the brisk manner of Stute.

"Yes?"

"And there in front of me, by the side of the road, I saw a motor-bike pulled up. As I got nearer the man who was sitting in the saddle said, "Hullo, Charlie," and I knew it was young Rogers."

"You couldn't see him though?"

"Enough to recognize him with his voice and all," said Meadows guardedly. "There was a young lady on the pillion seat."

"What sort of young lady?"

"I couldn't say. She was wearing a white mackintosh, that's all I know. The lights of the bike were in my eyes, so nothing was very clear."

"Did Rogers say anything else?"

"Yes, I'm coming to that. He asked what time the fast train left for London. 'This young lady,' he said, 'has to catch it.' So I told him at six o'clock. And he said, 'Thank you, Charlie. See you to-night.' And I went on."

"Oh. You did. What about him?"

"I didn't really notice. I was just getting near my cottage and was soon inside. It was too cold to hang about."

"And the girl never spoke?"

"Not while I was there."

"I see. Thank you, Meadows. Much obliged to you."

"That's all right," said Meadows, almost as disappointed as Mr. Sawyer had been at the laconic reception given to his tale. "Sorry I can't tell you any more."

When he had left us Stute drew paper and pen to him, and said, "Now then," in a peremptory way.

We waited. He seemed to be thinking deeply for a moment, then he began speaking, and, almost at the same time, writing.

"We can draw up some sort of a programme of what young Rogers did that day. There are some gaps in it, and it is dependent on the words of witnesses who may be mistaken or who may be lying. But it's some sort of plan to go on. And it's not bad for one day's work."

I noticed that he ignored altogether the day that Beef had put in before he arrived. This was, as far as I can remember, what he wrote:—

10.30. Left old Rogers's shop in Braxham.
11.0. Arrived at Rose Cottage, Chopley, and asked for Smythe.
11.5. Left Chopley.
1.0. Arrived at Riverside Private Hotel for lunch with Fairfax.

2.0.	Left Riverside Private Hotel with Fairfax.
2.10.	Reached the Mitre with Fairfax.
2.20.	On entrance of foreigner, left Mitre with Fairfax.
2.45.	Was starting up his motor-bike in the drive of Riverside Hotel.
4.0.	Arrived again at Rose Cottage.
4.0–5.0.	With Smythe at Rose Cottage.
5.10.	Bought rope in general store at Chopley.
5.50.	On road just outside Braxham speaking to Meadows.
6.10.	Entered Dragon public house near the station.
6.30.	Left the Dragon.
8.0.	Returned to Old Rogers's shop.
8.20.	Reached Mitre where he confessed to murder, and took poison.

"Do you see any flaws in that, Sergeant?" asked Stute.

"No, sir. Not so far as wot we've been told's concerned I don't. But of course there's some narsty gaps."

"Quite right. There are. Suppose we allow half an hour each time for his journey to Chopley. It couldn't take him much more, unless he had engine trouble, or was delayed in some other way. That means that there's an hour and twenty-five minutes unaccounted for between his leaving Chopley in the morning, and reaching Riverside. Then again if it takes ten minutes to walk from Riverside to the Mitre. . . ."

"No more, it wouldn't," put in Beef.

"Well, *you* should know, Sergeant," said Stute.

"I always bicycles," returned Beef.

"Anyway, say ten minutes. That leaves a quarter of an hour left blank between the time he walked out of the Mitre with Fairfax to the time he started up his motor-bike in the drive. And another three-quarters of an hour which we can't explain between then and the time he reached Rose Cottage."

"True enough," said Beef after a long examination of the 'time-table.'

"But what is most unaccountable," said Stute, "is the hour and a half between the time he left the Dragon, and his arrival at old Rogers's shop."

"Yes. That *is* funny," agreed Beef, stifling a yawn.

"However," said Stute, "patience and system. We'll fill it all in with time."

I rose to go, for it was getting near dinner-time, and I was tired and hungry. I turned to Stute.

"Thank you so much," I said, "for letting me come round with you to-day."

"Oh, that's all right," he returned with something approaching a smile, "We're used to that, you know. A crime wouldn't be a crime nowadays without half a dozen of you literary people hanging about after it. Why only the other day . . . But perhaps I'd better not tell you about her. She'd put me in her new book. Good night."

D

The Sergeant followed me to the door. With a mysterious nod backwards in the direction of Stute, he began to whisper hoarsely.

"'E's staying at the Mitre, where you are. So I shan't go in there to-night. If you wants a game of darts after you've 'ad your supper, come on down to the Dragon, and I'll see you three 'undred an' one up. See?"

I saw.

CHAPTER XII

I ACCEPTED Beef's invitation, and after a cold meal, set out for the Dragon. As I passed the alley running down beside it to the river, I paused to wonder why this had so much interested Stute. His orders that the Common should be searched argued that he imagined that the murder had been committed there. Why, then, his close scrutiny of this place, and his exclamation when he had seen the landing-stage? Had this been the fruit of an earlier theory, since exploded? Or had this place seen some other aspect of the tragedy? Or was it possible that the garrulous Mrs. Walker was right when she said that there might have been more than one murder?

Certainly the alley looked sinister enough, with the high walls of the warehouse looming over it. And I supposed that a body could have been dropped from that landing-stage into the river. But . . . well, I knew too much about investigation to start speculating.

Beef arrived a few minutes after I did, and we leaned over the bar. When Mr. Sawyer had satisfied his more insistent customers, he came up to us.

"There *was* something else I could have told you to-day," he said, and eyed us blearily.

"Wot's that?" asked Beef.

"Well, I didn't see why I should tell that other fellow. I didn't like him at all."

"'E's all right," said Beef. "Clever, too. You orter see 'ow 'e's worked out all wot young Rogers was up to on Wednesday. Got it all out with the times he was there and everythink. Course, 'e's used to it. A case like this isn't nothink to those chaps. 'E'll 'ave it all taped in next to no time."

"I daresay. But I didn't like him," repeated Mr. Sawyer obstinately. "He didn't seem to want to hear what anyone had got to tell him. And as I say, there was something else."

Beef sucked his moustache and tried to look interested.

"It was about young Rogers when he came here that evening. Swearing about you something dreadful, Sergeant."

"About *me*?"

"Yes. It appeared he hadn't got a rear-light on his motor-bike. That was why he took it down the alley instead of leaving it out the front. Only I wasn't going to tell that other fellow that. And he was saying that he wasn't going to give you a chance of making him pay a fine. Said you'd got a down on him. But he'd like to get his own back."

"Is that all?"

"Yes. That's all. Only I thought you ought to know."

Mr. Sawyer was called away to serve, but when he returned he asked how the case was going.

"If you don't mind," said Beef, with that absurd pomposity of his, "we won't discuss nothink about it. I 'ave enough of these things in the day-time without being 'arassed with them at night. A man must have *some* life of his own."

But when a few minutes later the obese Mr. Sawyer said he'd just thought of something else, the Sergeant showed interest again.

"It was when he was going off," said Mr. Sawyer. "He was all dressed up in his motor-biking things and they were wet. He looked up at the clock and said he'd have to hurry. He was meeting his girl at seven o'clock he said."

"He did, did he?" said Beef.

"Yes. It must have been about half an hour after he had come in, I should think."

"Thank you, Mr. Sawyer," said Beef.

An hour or two later, when I was in bed at the Mitre, I thought of the grotesque Sawyer wheezing out his trivial secret. That, I thought, was one reason why I liked following an investigation. It lifted the lid from a little town like Braxham, as nothing else could. With licence to ask the most personal and pertinent questions, the investigator could peep into a number of very divergent lives.

There was that fat publican for instance, waddling through day after day, rotting his in'ards with alcohol taken without fresh air or exercise to balance its effect, rising daily to open his dirty premises, sleeping stertorously, moving as little as possible, his brain stupefied by fumes, his eyes glazed. Lord knows what sort of a young man he had been—he was unimaginable in a form other than his present. And so he would stump on, until they had to carry his huge bloated carcase to burial.

How many other characters and stories had already been revealed by our two days' questioning! The old Rogers couple, who had adopted a ne'er-do-well tramp, because in their own words they had "taken to him" when he had come to their shop to beg. They were, the postman had said, "crazy" about the young man, and I could well believe it when I remembered Mrs. Rogers's tear-stained face, and the little bootmaker's worried look. Up to a point the fellow seemed to have responded—for at least he had preferred work to imposing on the kindness they would have been only too ready to show him.

One could see so well—now—what life had been like to the old couple in their neat home behind the shop. It was dominated by the calendar, and the date on which "Alan" was due for his few days' leave. I was almost inclined to agree with Molly Cutler when she said that young Rogers must have killed in self-defence. How else could he have faced the old people?

And the Cutlers, mother and daughter. What a curious conflict had been there. The older woman studying appearances, respectable, uncharitable—the girl lovely and free. One could see how she treated her mother—not with argument or aggression, but with a kind of secret indifference. She had never troubled to answer any of Mrs. Cutler's ill-natured references, yet she had her own point of view. One felt that up to a point the two had agreed to differ, and, when possible, had met on what common ground they had. It wasn't so much that Molly had concealed her love-affair from her mother. She had not discussed it, any more than she had discussed other intimate aspects of her life.

Yet she had been in love with young Rogers. There was no doubt about that. A deep and steadfast love, I thought, which had forgiven him much, and would have done much for him. What a fool the fellow had been not to have married her long ago. Unless there was some barrier of which we knew nothing.

I thought of Mrs. Murdoch, too, with her grim pretentiousness, her insistence on the use of words like "client," "lunch," "waiter," in speaking of her business, and yet the rather cheerless look of her hotel. She was the sort of woman who, if she knew more than she had already admitted, would cheerfully have lied rather than involve her hotel's name in unwelcome publicity.

Then Mrs. Walker. I thought with a smile how much of her tawdry self she had revealed. How she had been so ready to give young Rogers's address to the enquiring Miss Smythe, and how she had gloated over the situation when the girl had come down to "get her due." From all her garrulity nothing had emerged so clearly as the gusto with which she had watched the affair, and the chagrin she had felt at not being instantly made the chief witness. I could see her now, with her untidy red hair and not over-clean face as she poured out her precious information.

There were others who had shewn unexpected side to their natures. Mrs. Simmons, of this hotel, with her tip-toe respect for the presence of a dead body, even if it was a murderer's body; Mr. Simmons with his instantly selfish concern for its effect on his house; Charlie Meadows, delighted to have his little part in the investigation, and the waiter at Riverside yielding to Beef's "come off of it."

None of these people would ever have been more to me than passers-by, but the sudden earthquake in their town which a murder had caused had scattered their conventional covering wide.

It was, of course, too early to form a theory about the actual crime, and there were too many questions unanswered. If, for instance, young Rogers had indeed killed the girl, as it would seem reasonable to suppose, when had he done it? Not, as we had half-imagined, on the Common that afternoon, for she had been seen sitting on the back of his motor-bike at ten to six near the station. And how or where could he have done it after that? If she had *not* gone on the six o'clock train, where had she been during the twenty minutes or more that he spent in the Dragon, from 6.10 onwards? Or again, supposing that he had killed the girl, why had the Fairfaxes disappeared? And the foreigner?

Imagining the girl out of it, and picking Fairfax as the person murdered, when could

Rogers have done that? Had he taken the man out on the back of his motor-bike, and during that short time between starting up his motor-bike at Riverside and arriving at Rose Cottage, murdered him and disposed of the corpse? Almost impossible. Had Fairfax remained away from Riverside all the afternoon and been murdered by Rogers after the latter had seen Smythe on her train at six o'clock? If so, where? How? And, above all, why?

As for the foreigner, it was too obscure. We had no hint even of his nationality, certainly not of his reason for being in Braxham. But suppose young Rogers had killed him, afternoon or evening, who was it that I saw standing across the road when Beef and Simmons were carrying the corpse? Who had visited the corpse that night, and why?

It was all very well for Stute to talk about his system and his time-table, let him answer a few of these questions. Why, good heavens, we were as much in the dark as ever. We didn't even know young Rogers's real name.

CHAPTER XIII

DETECTIVE-INSPECTOR STUTE scarcely said good morning, when I reached the station next day, before he referred with some irritation to Beef.

"Not here yet!" he said. "The man has no sense of time." He gave me a rather grim smile. "You've spoiled him, you know, writing up the bit of luck he had in that Thurston case. The poor chap thinks he's a detective."

"I don't think he's ever thought that," I returned.

Just then Beef entered, looking somewhat dazed and irritable, as he is apt to do in the early morning.

"Well, Sergeant," said Stute, "I've done half a day's work. I've given instructions in London that every effort shall be made to find the girl Smythe's address or to trace her story before this happened. If she is what we suppose it shouldn't be hard to find out where her room was, though whether she's still alive or not remains to be seen."

His brisk voice went on, as he turned over the papers before him.

"I've also arranged for the Common to be searched, at any rate for two hundred yards each side of the road to begin with. They will form search parties out there. Fortunately the hunting instinct is still strong enough in human beings to make the formation of a search party an easy matter."

Stute paused and lit a cigarette.

"Then—are you listening, Sergeant?—I have sent for the postman who delivers in the High Street to come here as soon as he's finished his round."

"Wotever d'you want 'im for?" These were the first words Beef had spoken.

"I want to see whether any other letters were delivered to young Rogers of which his aunt and uncle knew nothing. An ordinary routine enquiry, Beef. The sort of enquiry you ought to have made already. I wish you could realize that a case like this is not cleared up by some miraculous flash of insight or deduction, but by a steady accumulation of the facts."

"Yessir," said Beef.

"Then, since I gather you had forgotten the matter, I have given orders for the searching of the interior of that warehouse beside the Dragon."

"Oh yes. I get you," said Beef, sucking his moustache.

"And finally, I had a look at the motor-bike. I understand that you have allowed it to remain at old Rogers's. I had it brought round. It should have been brought here at once."

"Why? There was nothink to see. I 'ad a look at it."

"That is for me to judge, Sergeant. And now, will you kindly attend while I tell you what reports have come in this morning? Thank you. The Research Department tell us that the stains on the cuff of the shirt and the sleeve of the coat are actually the stains of human blood. The bottle from which young Rogers drank contained cyanide of potassium. And the Fairfax couple have not yet been traced."

"Well, we knew about the stains and the bottle," said Beef, "so we aren't much forrader."

"Wait a minute," said Stute. "I have a report here from a man who examined the only one of young Rogers's fellow stewards who had anything revelant to say."

Beef looked up. This seemed to interest him.

"Only one little point emerges," said Stute, "and it's this. Young Rogers was apparently in the habit of bringing home a number of tickets for the Buenos Aires Lottery. He had them in a sealed envelope, and told this steward that he was always a bit afraid they would be found on him by the Customs officers."

"'S' that all?"

"Yes. Our man tried hard to get anything further there might be, but Rogers had never told him what he did with the tickets in England."

"Well, that's worth knowing, anyway," said Beef.

"Everything connected with the case is worth knowing," said Stute. "It is by co-ordinating all these pieces of information that we shall arrive at the truth."

There was a knock at the door, and Constable Galsworthy came in. There was an air of respectful independence about this big, finely-built countryman, with the ruddy young face and rather intelligent eyes, which made me inclined to support his claim for consideration as an efficient policeman, as against that of Constable Smith of Chopley, who had been almost ingratiating towards Stute.

"Fawcett, the postman, is here, sir," he said to Stute.

"Show him in," said the detective.

Fawcett looked a little embarrassed as he took a chair. His encounters with Beef were usually less formal.

"I want you, Fawcett, to think carefully. Can you remember what letters you have delivered for young Rogers lately?"

Fawcett thought carefully. "There was one," he said at last.

"When did it arrive?"

"I can't say exactly. A day or so before he got home."

"You didn't notice the postmark?"

"No. I didn't. If I had to notice every postmark on the letters I deliver—well."

"Nor the handwriting?"

"No."

"And you can't remember any others lately?"

"No."

"None from abroad?"

This query caused Fawcett to think carefully again.

"There *was* one from abroad," he said at last, "but I don't think it was for him. It was for Mr. Rogers."

"When did that arrive?"

"Before the other one. I should say about a week before. I remember that because it was one of those thin envelopes what they use for air mail."

"Indeed? You are sure it wasn't for young Rogers?"

"Not so far as I can remember. I have an idea—can't be sure, mind you—that it was just addressed to 'Mr. Rogers' and nothing more. But that may be my fancy."

"You remember delivering it?"

"Yes. Because I said to Mr. Rogers that you want to be careful of them thin envelopes in case they get lost among the others."

"He took it himself."

"That's right."

"And where had it come from?"

"Ah. Now you're asking," said Fawcett. "I don't know nothing about foreign postage." He implied that he was nothing less than an authority on the home variety. "I can only say this came from abroad."

"Well, I'm much obliged to you, Fawcett. That's all we shall require."

And Fawcett, though he couldn't afterwards have explained his reason for it, said, "Thank you, sir," and left.

Stute was uncharacteristically silent and thoughtful for a moment, then he said, "Might be worth following up. Send me that constable with the ridiculous name, Beef."

"Galsworthy!" Beef shouted without rising from his chair.

Stute winced but turned to the young man. "Go round to Mr. Rogers, the bootmaker, and ask him if he remembers a letter arriving by air mail from abroad about a week before his adopted nephew came home. Find out who had written it, and to whom it was addressed, and anything else you can. And by the way, I would like a specimen of young Rogers's handwriting."

"Very good, sir."

Once more we were alone.

My recollection of the whole of that day, in fact, is of spending hours in Beef's little office, with Stute receiving reports and sending out enquiries. It was a day for trimming the edges of our evidence, and squeezing out the last detail from local informants. Before mid-day the man who had searched the warehouse returned to say that he had found nothing. It was Beef's second constable who had done this job, a rather lanky young man, with a large nose, called Curtis.

"There was nothing there, sir," he said quite coolly to Stute, to whom he was making his report, "and you can take it that unless anyone had a key and went in from the door that opens on to the street, no one has been there. There was dust and cobwebs round the windows and doors on the river side which hadn't been disturbed for months."

"And nothing *in* the place?"

"Nothing at all, sir."

"Thank you, Curtis."

Stute never showed any sign of disappointment when he drew blank. And he had another disappointment a few minutes later when Galsworthy returned from the bootmaker's.

"Well?" he snapped at the constable.

"I saw Mr. Rogers, sir," began Galsworthy rather breathlessly, "and he remembered the letter perfectly. It *was* to him, he says, and had been sent by young Rogers himself from Rio de Janeiro on the way home."

"Did you ask him what it was about?"

"Yessir. Nothing special, he said. It appears that young Rogers had the habit of sending them an air mail letter now and again when he was out there. Mr. Rogers looked to see if he'd kept it, but he hadn't. He found an old envelope addressed in young Rogers's writing and gave it to me. Here you are, sir."

We examined a dirty envelope. The writing was firm and straight, not altogether the writing of an illiterate man, but not ornate or scholarly.

"Very well, constable," said Stute. He still could not bring himself to enunciate the name.

The next person to be shown in brought us more satisfying information. He was the Vicar of Chopley, a boisterous and professedly busy individual, rubicund and noisy.

"Ah, Inspector," he shouted to Stute, and I silently wondered why parsons so frequently opened their sentences with that sound, "young Smith, our village policeman at Chopley, suggested that I should give you a call."

His tones rang through the whole police station. I was thankful to see that Stute treated him with no more ceremony than he had shewn to other informants.

"Sit down, Vicar," said Stute.

"Fact is, I may be able to help you in this tragic business. Or then again my information may be useless. But I was talking to young Smith—he used to be one of my choirboys, you know; smart young fellow, and I hope he gets on." My personal championship of Galsworthy against Smith was instantly strengthened. "I was telling him that I was returning from Braxham on Wednesday afternoon in my car. . . ."

"What time would that have been?"

"Time? Time? Ha! Ha! You ask me what time! You don't know my reputation, Inspector. Most unpunctual fellow in the world. I'm notorious for it. Time means nothing to me."

"Still, about?"

"Well, it must have been between five and six in the afternoon. I was alone at the time. And I happened to see a motor-bike standing by the roadside."

"Facing which way?"

"Towards me. Towards Braxham."

"What make?"

"Ah! There I *can* help you. Used to be a great motor-cyclist. Had to give it up now, of course. It was a Rudge-Whitworth. The 500 c.c. Special type. I should say fairly new. Well, I thought, the usual thing. Young people, Inspector, young people!" And he gave a laugh which I suppose might be described as hearty, but to me sounded almost macabre.

"Did you see anyone?"

"Indeed I did. A young man and a girl. They were walking away from me across the

Common. I couldn't see their faces. But the fellow wore one of those black oilskin outfits complete with leggings. And the girl had a white mackintosh. Of course I drove straight on."

"Of course." Stute rose before his visitor. "Very much obliged to you, Vicar."

"Not at all. Delighted. Wish I could tell you more. Tricky job, yours. Ha! Ha! Got the murderer and can't find the murder! Well I never! Good day, Inspector!" And he shouted himself out of the building.

It was then about three o'clock, and Stute elected that we should drive at once to the Common and see how the search party had progressed. The Vicar's statement seemed to be an additional indication that hopes of discovery lay in that area. However noisy and disturbing his personality, his information was very much to the point. There was no mistaking his description of the clothes worn by Rogers and Smythe, and the girl. He had even noticed the make of the motor-bike.

There seemed to me to be a good chance that we might be going straight to a solution. I was glad that Stute drove fast and that Constable Smith of Chopley was awaiting us.

"I concentrated the search in the part the Vicar showed me," he said.

"Found anything?"

"Quite a lot," answered Smith, with a self-satisfied smile, and began leading us towards a collection of objects laid out on the grass.

Stute frowned. "What on earth's all this?" he asked.

A curious miscellany was displayed. Old boots, paper bags, the remains of a woman's skirt, a newspaper, tins, two kettles (one spoutless), a man's hat, a rusted pen-knife, and a child's doll. But almost every one of these articles had quite evidently been on the Common at least since the previous summer, possibly for years. The boots were almost historical, the skirt might have served several seasons ago for a gypsy, the tins and the pen-knife were hopelessly rusted, the hat a mere relic, the doll in a worse condition than the one found by the sentimental lady whose song enlivens Charles Kingley's *Water-Babies*.

"Good heavens, Smith," said Stute angrily.

"Thought I better collect all there was, sir."

"The man's a fool," remarked Stute, to my great pleasure.

But Smith was smiling. "I found this, too," he said, "it was near a few sodden ashes of burnt paper." And he handed Stute a small fragment of a Ms. Peeping over his shoulder I saw:

> you know I
> always, but
> Stella, when
> never. We
> but not
> please

It was in young Rogers's handwriting.

PART TWO

CHAPTER XIV

THE inquest had taken place some days ago, and had revealed nothing new. The investigation, in fact, had become almost hum-drum, for there had been no discovery which could be described as startling since that priggish young Constable Smith of Chopley had found a fragment of young Rogers's letter.

But Stute stayed on in Braxham, and since he was putting up at the Mitre, where I always stayed, we saw a good deal of one another, and had become quite close acquaintances. I liked the man. He was thoroughly efficient, and behind his brisk manner there was a kind of humanity which one could respect. I had complete confidence in his capabilities, and knew that it was only a question of time before he solved this peculiar problem.

I no longer went round with him and Beef, nor followed all their researches in person, but Stute and I usually dined together in the evening, and he was glad of someone to talk to about the case. "Poor old Beef's all very well," he used to say, "but there are some points of psychology which one could scarcely expect him to follow." So over our meal, Stute would give me a curt outline of their progress, and I was duly appreciative.

One evening he more or less summed matters

up in a long statement of the case as he saw it.
I could see that he was expounding it largely
in order to get his own ideas clear, for there is
nothing like a verbal exposition of facts to make
them coherent to the speaker. But I did not
mind in the least being used as an audience.
I, too, wanted to get the thing less jumbled in
my mind.

"There are," said Stute, "so far as we have
reason to know at present, four main possibilities.
One, that Rogers murdered Smythe. Two, that
Rogers murdered Fairfax. Three, that Rogers
murdered the foreigner. And four, that Rogers
only believed that he had murdered someone,
and had actually done nothing of the sort. I
don't think we need seriously consider the
possibility of his having murdered more than
one person. But since it is not mathematically
certain that he did not do so, you can call that
number five if you like.

"Now against every one of those possibilities,
there is something which seems almost to preclude
it. Take the girl first. We know that he took
her away from Chopley. We know that he stopped
on the Common and walked away with her.
But then we know that no corpse was found on
the Common, for I've now had the whole area
thoroughly searched. And we know that he
was seen not far from Braxham station with her,
at ten to six.

"I've cross-examined the station staff, but
they can't tell me whether the girl travelled on
the six o'clock or not. Quite natural. It's a
fast train and fairly crowded. They can't

remember seeing young Rogers at the station, but they agree that he might easily have been there without their noticing him. There was no taxi waiting outside to see him arrive on his motor-bike. In fact no evidence one way or the other.

"Suppose, then, that she did not travel, but was murdered. The only time, it seems, that he had in which to murder her was between ten to six and ten past, for at ten past he entered the Dragon alone. And the only possible place would be in the alley beside the Dragon, or on the landing-stage of the factory. But both those seem fantastic to me. It would be virtually out of the question for him to persuade her to follow him down that alley, and stab her there. For one thing, there would have been the risk, if not the certainty, of her screaming, and raising the alarm, for it was within a few yards of the back windows of the Dragon. For another thing, how could he have persuaded her to accompany him there? And for another there could scarcely have been time, for Sawyer the publican heard him come up on his motor-bike and enter the bar without enough delay to attract his notice.

"There are two other ways in which he might have murdered Smythe. He might have done it *after* 6.40. But then what did he do with her while he was in the Dragon? She was not at all the sort of girl to share our good Beef's views on a woman's attitude towards a public house. *She* would never have waited patiently for him while he went in for a drink. And although I've had the most exhaustive enquiry made in the town I can find no one who saw a girl in a white mackintosh on Wednesday evening at all. And anyway, why should she have stayed in Braxham at that time? I admit that this is not wholly off the cards. She *might* have waited for him somewhere while he was in the Dragon. He *might* have killed her later. But somehow the chance of it seems too small to be considered.

"The other chance of Smythe having been the victim at first looked better to me. It was that the girl seen by Meadows on the back of the motor-bike at 5.50 was not Smythe at all, but another girl wearing her white mackintosh and impersonating her. That would mean that Rogers had already murdered Smythe somewhere between Chopley and Braxham, or within a short distance of the route, and was deliberately working an alibi—by trying to prove that she was alive at 5.50. But that doesn't hold water. For one reason, I am convinced that his only other woman friend was Molly Cutler, and at 5.50 she was sitting at high tea with her mother. And again, what could he have done with the corpse? He had had only forty-five minutes to cover the ten miles from Chopley, do his murder, conceal the body, and meet his accomplice. Again, impossible, especially since that walk across the Common had to be taken into account, and there was certainly no body near the part in which it took place. Besides, it would mean that the whole thing had been most intricately timed and planned, if he was to have someone ready to wear the disguising mackintosh and sit on his pillion at that point and time, to establish an alibi. So altogether, I don't see how the victim can have been Smythe.

"But when we come to the others, there are just as many objections. Take Fairfax. He was last seen leaving the Mitre with Rogers at 2.20. At four o'clock Rogers arrives at Rose Cottage, quite cheerful and ready to discuss with Smythe the return of his letters. Now could the man who later felt so guilty about his crime that he confessed to it and committed suicide, have gone through that hour with Smythe, appeared normal to Mrs. Walker, greeted Meadows and later drank with Sawyer, having just committed a murder? It is ridiculous. If he murdered Fairfax it must have been in the evening, after he had made all those arrangements with Smythe unconscious of any possibility that he would be a murderer before the night. And if he murdered Fairfax in the evening, where had Fairfax been from 2.20 onwards? No one in the town remembers seeing him, though he was a well-known figure. And he never returned to his hotel.

"Again, if it was Fairfax he murdered, where is Mrs. Fairfax? And why hasn't she raised an outcry about her husband's absence? We know that she had no hand in the murder, even supposing that she was party to it, for she spent Wednesday afternoon and evening in town with Mrs. Rogers. Why haven't we heard from her?

"Then the foreigner. I grant you that this might seem to be the best chance, but even so it leaves too much to be explained to be convincing. Who was this foreigner, and what was his interest in young Rogers? Was he the person who had been following him? Those points may be cleared up by our report from Buenos Aires, when it comes. But even so, if it was the foreigner who was murdered by Rogers, who was the man you saw watching the removal of the corpse? You described him as looking 'foreign.' And Mrs. Watt, who took Molly Cutler home that evening, has been to us to report that a 'foreign looking man' who spoke very bad English was hanging about outside. She says he asked her what had taken place and that she didn't reply. That would mean, then, that there were two foreigners in the district which seems scarcely likely when we cannot find any trace of even one's having stayed a night in Braxham.

"To raise another more fanciful supposition—suppose Rogers and Fairfax had actually shared some motive for wanting to rid themselves of this 'foreigner' and had murdered him together, and that Fairfax had impersonated the foreigner to Mrs. Watt, and to you—what object could he have had? Was he hoping that we should assume *him* to have been the murdered man? It's out of the question, for he could not have known that young Rogers wouldn't tell us whom he had murdered before taking poison.

"Then, lastly, there's the possibility I mentioned that young Rogers only believed he had killed someone, and that the person whom he believed dead is even now recovering secretly from his attack. Well, I suppose this might be the explanation. But most of my objections to the other theories apply to this—except the ones that refer to the concealment of the corpse, of course. And that person, whoever he or she is, must be pretty badly wounded. A fellow like Rogers would have good reason before he committed suicide. He was certain in his mind, at any rate, that his victim was dead, when he swallowed that poison. How, then, could a seriously wounded person have been got out of Braxham, or have been kept *in* Braxham for that matter, and treated for wounds, without our hearing of it? No, I don't much like that theory either. Not at present, anyway.

"So you see, Townsend, we are still in a fog. But little by little the facts are coming in. And one only needs enough relevant facts to form a theory, and enough confirmation of a theory to make a case. So we keep at it."

"You do," I said with some admiration, "and you certainly put what you have got very lucidly. It will straighten out in time—it must do. For one thing, one or another of the three people will turn up, which will narrow down your search."

"Yes," said Stute, "it seems that our best chance is a system of elimination, and then concentration on the remaining suspect. Suspect of being murdered, of course," he added with a smile.

"What does old Beef say about it?"

Stute chuckled. "The Sergeant has got very reserved lately," he said, "and from hints dropped here and there I have an idea that he has a theory of his own. You've got a lot to answer for, Townsend. But I rather like the old chap. He's conscientious, anyway."

CHAPTER XV

BUT a few nights later, Stute was much more cheerful. He sat down at the small table we shared, and before Mrs. Simmons had had time to bring the soup he tossed a few sheets of type-script on the table.

"Well, Townsend," he said, "what do you think of that? It is a translation of the report I received to-day by air mail from Comisario Julio Mareno Mendez of Buenos Aires. I met him some years ago at the International Police Conference of New York."

"Who is he?" I asked.

"He's the officer in charge of the Sección Identificaciones of the Argentine Police. All the finger-print archives are in his care. A most intelligent fellow."

I began to read the document which Stute had handed to me.

"Sección Identificaciones,
"Division Investigaciones,
"Policia de la Capital Federal.
"Buenos Aires,
"Rep. ARGENTINA.

"ESTEEMED COLLEAGUE,

"It gives me the greatest pleasure to recall our acquaintance in New York, and to be able to show you by the sincerity of my present greetings, that even our work, surrounded by sordid circumstances as so often it is, gives scope now and again for a friendly salutation across the ocean, and a means of co-operating one with another in the object which we both faithfully serve—the combating of crime. It will be my endeavour and pleasure to answer your queries as fully as the means in my power and the considerable bulk of information collected by the department which I have the honour to direct, enable me to do.

"You ask me whether we know anything of a compatriot of yours, Alan Rogers, a steward employed on the Line of steamers running between Britain and Buenos Aires. I have had pleasure in making the most detailed and assiduous enquiries in our Section of Robberies and Damages, in our Section of Frauds and Swindles, in our Section of Personal Security, in that of Special Laws, and in that of Social Order. From these enquiries I am able to tell you that the subject Alan Rogers was under direct suspicion of being involved in drug smuggling and that a warrant had actually been issued for his arrest, and would have been put into action during his next visit to our country. Our Immigration Section had received orders to go aboard the ship to work, and arrest him, immediately this ship came into port. We had reason to know that the subject Alan Rogers was acting as a go-between for powerful miscreants engaged in this traffic, though we have so far been unable to discover the identity either of the perpetrators of this crime over here, or the malefactors with whom they were in communication in your country. We believe, however, that cocaine was being carried by Rogers from the dastardly gang for whom he worked in Buenos Aires, to equally unscrupulous but no less powerful persons in your territory.

"In this connection I am instructed to say that the Police of the Federal Capital will be profoundly grateful to His Britannic Majesty's Police for any information which the latter may be able to give them about the associates of the subject Alan Rogers in England, in the hope that from this information may arise the evidence they need in their indefatigable pursuit of the corresponding criminals in Buenos Aires.

"Now with regard to the two sets of finger-prints which you have sent us, one of the right hand and one of the left, of a male person, I am pleased to be able to tell you that we have identified these. I should like to remind you, esteemed colleague, of the conversation which we had on the subject of finger-prints on the pleasant occasion of our meeting in New York. I explained to you then our unique system of classification (embracing practically the whole population, not only persons under arrest, as in your country), and assured you, somewhat to your amusement, I remember, that here in Buenos Aires, by the Vucetich System, we were, on occasion, able to make the dead speak, or at any rate pronounce in unmistakable and infallible

E

terms, their own identities. This seemed to you at the time, I recall, too large a claim for me to make for our archives, and for our principle of cataloguing finger-prints according to their own characteristics, so that the man might be identified from his finger-prints, and not only the finger-prints of a given man sought in the police library, as in your no doubt estimable system. I cannot resist the temptation to point out that this is actually a case in point, and that from our archives we have been able, with no information but the finger-prints themselves, to identify the possessor. And I would like to have the temerity to express the hope that at some time in the future your excellent, efficient, modern and brilliant directors at Scotland Yard may perceive the fact that a system which is able to perform this is unsurpassable.

"The man whose finger-prints you send me is Charles Riley, born in 1900 at Bristol, who was arrested in Buenos Aires seven years and three months ago on a charge of assault and battery and resistance to the police. It was on the occasion of this arrest that his finger-prints were taken and filed. The subject Charles Riley was employed at this time in a similar capacity to that of the subject Alan Rogers, but on the —— Line of steamships which run from Buenos Aires to New York. He received a sentence of two months' imprisonment, at the end of which he was deported to his native country of England, and forbidden re-entry to this country. We have no reason for supposing that Riley and

Rogers are in fact the same person, but we have no reason for supposing the contrary, as we have no finger-prints as yet of Rogers.

"May I express the ardent hope that the information I have fortunately been able to have the honour of conveying to you may be of direct assistance to you in whatever investigation may be occupying you at this moment.

"I salute you attentively,

"Your colleague and friend,

"JULIO MARENO MENDEZ."

"Phew!" I said, overcome by this exuberance.

"You must remember," Stute said at once, "that it is translated literally from Spanish, the most courtly language in the world. And the point is that his information is accurate and to the point, and clears up a number of our mysteries."

"What does Beef think of it?" I asked.

Stute smiled. "The Sergeant, in his own words, is 'took aback.' He 'wouldn't never have believed it possible.' I'm afraid that to Beef anything that is really and thoroughly methodical must always seem more or less miraculous. I left him trying to pronounce the name Julio Mareno Mendez in a sort of ecstasy of admiration."

"Well, I don't altogether wonder. It is pretty marvellous. So now you know young Rogers's real name."

"Yes. And we know how he came to be down-and-out when he went to beg from old Rogers in Bromley that day. And we know what his envelope of 'lottery tickets' really contained. And we can form a pretty good guess at his business with Fairfax."

"And the foreigner?"

Stute considered. "I think," he said, "if we find out just who Mr. Fairfax was, whether he's alive or dead, we shall have some more ideas about that foreigner."

"Yes," I agreed, "but for all that this report tells you about young Rogers, it doesn't tell you anything directly indicative of the identity of the person he murdered."

"Directly, no. You mustn't expect things to come directly. I tell you that detection is nothing but the collection and co-ordination of relevant facts. And my 'esteemed colleague' in Buenos Aires has given me some valuable ones."

I thought what admirable patience and coolness the man had. He had got a completely fresh line of research. Drug-smuggling, a wholly new and sinister element, had been brought into what had seemed a sordid tragedy in a small country town, but he saw nothing to get excited about. His keen mind was busy with the jig-saw as it now appeared.

"Of course," he said presently, "I've been in touch with the Yard. They are looking up to see if Charles Riley has any sort of record, for strange as it would seem to Señor Julio Mareno Mendez, we also have our archives, even if our finger-prints are *not* catalogued on the Vucetich system."

"Of course," I said.

"And I've got an entirely new line of research

on Fairfax. I've asked them to see if they can link him up with any known drug-pedlar. I shouldn't be at all surprised if enquiries in *that* direction brought results."

"No. It looks promising."

"All the same, we mustn't let all this drug theory blind us to the possibility that it may, after all, have been the girl he murdered, and this turn out to be a mere side-line in crime of the fellow's. It's strange what you stir up when you begin to look into people's lives."

CHAPTER XVI

I WENT down the High Street next day to buy
some razor-blades, and was turning towards my
hotel when I saw Molly Cutler coming towards
me, alone. I was not forgetful of my responsi-
bilities as chronicler to Sergeant Beef. There
were evident precedents for me. Gentlemen in
my rôle in the novels of detection I had so
avidly read, had frequently been rewarded by
becoming engaged to some lady involved, but
not too intimately involved, in one of the
master's cases. There was, of course, Dr. Watson,
who achieved a marriage of legendary happiness
in this way, and there was the conscientiously
short-sighted Captain Hastings. So, anxious to
do my best for Beef, I raised my hat.

Molly Cutler stopped and smiled, vaguely at
first, but then with recognition. "Oh yes," she
said, "you were with Sergeant Beef that day."

Her voice was tired and toneless, but she
looked no less attractive than she had done on
that first night when she had rushed in from the
rain, and thrown herself beside her lover's body.

"Have they discovered anything yet?" she
asked.

"Yes. Quite a lot. I wonder . . . would
you care to come in for a coffee?" And I
indicated a confectioner's shop with a tea-room
attached to it.

This drinking of coffee at eleven o'clock in the morning is a good English provincial habit. It is odd that whereas on the Continent the men spend their time in cafés and the women remain at home, in England it is the women who haunt these places while the men work. As I conducted Molly Cutler to a rather isolated table, we passed groups of local ladies busily sipping the creamy, hot, but very inferior coffee supplied in such places, or talking emphatically between their sips.

There were glances at my companion, and surreptitious efforts to attract attention to her. Women whose backs were turned twisted their faces to see "the girl in the case." There could be little doubt that her name had been on their lips before we entered.

"Thanks," said Molly as I held her chair. Then, turning to me, she asked at once what they had found out. She had been a witness at the inquest, of course, so that the only news I could give her was of discoveries which had not been made public. I told her of the piece of Rogers's letter, but hesitated when I came to the report from Buenos Aires.

"You know, Miss Cutler," I said, "I think you're wrong in worrying over Rogers. It's hard to tell you, but. . . ."

"Well?" She had turned swiftly and defiantly to me.

"As a matter of fact information has come through to Detective-Inspector Stute which shows . . . well, quite apart from this affair, he really was no good."

"Information? What information?" She sounded quite hostile now, and I wished that I hadn't put myself in this position.

"He's had a report from Buenos Aires. . . ."

Molly Cutler gave a rather bitter little laugh. "Oh, *that*," she said, "I know about that."

This was startling. "You knew. . . ."

"You mean about his having been in prison out there? And deported? And how he changed his name? He told me all about it. It was through a fight he got into with a Belgian. Alan was a terribly impulsive fellow. I'm afraid he was often in scrapes of that kind. But they meant nothing. This fellow insulted him, and he hit him harder than he meant to. Alan was arrested, and there you are."

She shrugged and looked down at her hands which were folded on the table.

"Yes. They told Stute about that in their report. But it wasn't that I meant when I said he was no good."

"Then what did you mean?"

I thought there was a touch of something between impatience and contempt in her voice.

"You won't be angry with me if I tell you?"

"With you? No. Why should I be?"

I'm sorry to say that this sounded rather as though she did not think me worth her anger. But I went on.

"Well, the Buenos Aires police were going to arrest Rogers when he landed there again. He had been drug-smuggling."

For a moment Molly stared straight at me. Then she flushed a little.

"That's nonsense, of course," she said briefly.

I shook my head. "For your sake, I wish it were. It seems to mean so much to you that this fellow's name shall be whitened. But there's every proof. Stute even has confirmation from a fellow steward of Rogers's, on his ship. There can't be much doubt of it."

She did not speak, and when she looked up again I saw that her eyes had tears in them which threatened to fall.

"What else are you people going to accuse him of?" she said at last, in a low intense voice. "Murder—and now drug-smuggling. You haven't the least idea what he was like."

"What *was* he like?" I asked, largely to keep her talking and save her, and me, from the embarrassment of a scene in this place.

"Alan had lots of faults," she said, "a violent temper was one of them. He drank too much, sometimes, and I suppose he had left a few debts behind him in different places. But there was nothing wicked in him."

"You can't conceive of his having smuggled cocaine into the country?"

"No. I can't. He would never have done it. It wasn't the kind of thing he did."

"So that—if he was doing it, you think he didn't know what he carried. Is that it?"

She looked a little less forbidding. "Yes! That must have been it. If he *was* doing it."

"And now tell me something else, Miss Cutler. Can you, honestly, conceive of young Rogers murdering anyone?"

She did not speak for a second. Then she looked up sharply.

"Are you trying to catch me?" she said.

"Catch you? Of course not. I . . . well, to tell you the truth, I was almost beginning to think of this man as you paint him. And I wanted to know. . . ."

"Well, then—I *can* conceive of Alan murdering someone. He was a violent sort of chap. But I don't believe he ever did it in a premeditated way. I don't believe he ever schemed to do it. If someone attacked him, or provoked him, he was capable of anything. But there was no subtlety in his nature."

"I think I believe you there," I said. "I believe that when we get at the truth you will turn out to have been right over that. But if that was so"—my inexpert mind had sudden misgivings—"why should he have committed suicide? He had everything to lose. He was engaged to you, and he had a good job. Surely if it was during a violent scene of some sort there would have been a chance for him to get off with manslaughter. How can you account for his having taken poison?"

"He had terrible fits of remorse over nearly everything crazy that he did. This must have been worse, that's all."

Somehow, in my mind, I was trying to make her conception of young Rogers conform with the facts that Stute and Beef possessed. Unconsciously, I suppose, I was trying to make her feel happier about it all. And suddenly I had an idea.

"Suppose," I said, "that he was made to believe he had committed murder. Suppose that some interested party had been able to convince him that he had been guilty of an act which in reality had been the work of another. That would account for it, wouldn't it?"

She stared at me blankly for a moment.

"My God!" she said at last, and I saw that she had turned pale, "that must have been it! What a wicked thing to do. *Could* anyone do that? Make him think he was guilty?"

"There are some people who have *no* scruples," I returned, rather tritely perhaps.

"How awful! So Alan poisoned himself because he thought he had committed a crime which someone else. . . . Oh, it's the most terrible thing!"

"But Miss Cutler, it was only an idea of mine. It may not have any truth in it."

"It has! It is true! I see it now! Oh, if only we had met that evening. And how do you suppose they did it—convinced him, I mean?"

"I don't know. I only mentioned it as a possibility. I am not a detective, and if I were I probably should never have considered that. Because, after all, there was the knife—his knife. How are you going to account for that? It had a bloodstain on it. So had his shirt-cuff and sleeve. Even if he didn't actually kill the person, he must have. . . ."

"Oh, don't . . ." she begged.

"I'm awfully sorry. Perhaps I should never have suggested the idea. That's the worst of anyone like me plunging about in a case of this sort."

I could see that her lip was trembling. Poor girl, these days must have been hideous for her. The thing itself, the inquest, the people in the town.

"Miss Cutler," I said, trying to speak considerately, "why don't you go away for a bit, while they're clearing this thing up. It can't do you any good to be here. You're making yourself more wretched than you need."

She shook her head. "No," she said, "I want to stay and see it all settled. I want to know the truth. It's not much I can do for him now, but I can do that. And I will."

"I think you are very brave—and loyal," I said quietly.

To my surprise and pleasure she was pleased at that. She even gave me a half smile.

"Thank you," she said. "And now. . . ."

She was interrupted by a voice behind my chair.

"Molly! Really, how very inconsiderate! I've been searching all over the town for you."

I rose to face her over-neat and disapproving-looking mother.

"Won't you sit down?" I asked.

"I suppose I shall have to, now that my daughter has brought me in here. Rather than cause more talk, I will. But it's not very pleasant for *me* to be in this place, with everyone staring at us."

Molly sighed and for the first time that I had heard, she had an answer to her mother.

"What does it matter whether they stare or not?" she asked wearily.

"It may not matter to you," said her mother. "You may be past such things. But it does to me. I've never in all my life given anyone cause to talk about me, and I'm not used to it. Yes, please, a cup of coffee. Yes, and perhaps it would look more natural if I had a cake. Thank you, one of those meringues will do nicely."

She was not too embarrassed by the attention which her daughter had attracted to cope very capably with a large cream meringue, a type of cake I have never been able to eat successfully.

"And there was something else that Molly ought to have told that policeman the other day," she went on when she had left only a few crumbs on her plate and one adhering obstinately to her chin.

"Mother!" her daughter broke in. Molly looked distressed.

"Yes. It should be known," said Mrs. Cutler primly, "this young man, this Rogers, once told Molly that if ever the *need* arose he didn't lack the *means* to commit murder."

"But of course he didn't. Who, as a matter of fact, does?" I returned, and I felt that Molly was pleased with my indifference.

As soon as Mrs. Cutler thought it expedient, she and her daughter got up and left the café. But Molly smiled sadly back to me.

CHAPTER XVII

I USED to have breakfast about an hour later than Stute and next morning, as I was finishing my toast and home-made marmalade, Constable Galsworthy was shown in by Mrs. Simmons. He looked almost offensively healthy and full of beans, and I remarked on it.

"I'm in training for the Police Boxing Championship," he explained. "I got into the final last year."

So that was it. I had always thought that he looked like a boxer. "Did you want to see me?" I asked.

"Yes, sir. Detective-Inspector Stute told me to call in on my way by. He's had a report in from Scotland Yard, and says that if you want to see the next move in this case, you had better go round there."

"The next move?" I repeated.

"That's what he said, sir."

"Well, thank you, Constable. I'll go straight round."

I hadn't had a chance to speak to Beef for some days, and was glad to see his red face, with a smile on it, when I entered his little office.

"Morning, Townsend," said Stute. "I thought you would like to hear the latest. We've had two reports about Fairfax."

He picked up a photograph of a heavy-faced, solemn, not very amiable-looking man, and handed it to me.

"His real name is, or was, Ferris," he said, "and he was convicted ten years ago of selling cocaine. So far as our people can make out, he scarcely bothered to allow a decent lapse to go by after he had come out of gaol before he was engaged in the same traffic."

"Makes you think, doesn't it," said Beef, growing philosophical. "I mean you never know what you're going to find out about anyone. 'Ere we are, investigating a suicide and confession of murder, and we come on this bloke selling drugs. I sometimes wonder whether if we was to look into anyone's doings, as close as we do when they been up to somethink like murder, we shouldn't find they'd all got skelingtons in their cupboards."

"Seems as though your 'esteemed colleague' in Buenos Aires was right about Rogers, anyway."

"Yes. I don't think we should be jumping to conclusions if we presumed that young Rogers was bringing drugs in for Fairfax. Unfortunately that doesn't tell us whether it was Fairfax whom he murdered, and if it wasn't, who was the victim. Which brings me to the second report."

We waited while Stute turned over his papers.

"It isn't very much, but it might help us. The woman tenant of the basement in the house where Fairfax, or Ferris, lived in Hammersmith suddenly took it into her head to remember the

firm which had moved their furniture there.
They had been in the flat about two years, so
this was lucky. But the firm was Pickertons,
which was not so lucky, as with a large firm
like that it is hard to trace a specified move. But
the manager was most helpful. He went through
his books very carefully, and discovered that the
furniture had been collected from a London
depository, and moved to Hammersmith for a
Mr. Freeman. And he was able to give our
man the name of the depository."

"See 'ow they do it?" said Beef gleefully.
"Wonderful 'ow they follow 'em up, isn't
it?"

"The depository took longer to find the
record, but eventually told us that they had
moved Mr. Freeman's things from the village
of Long Highbury in Oxfordshire."

Beef rubbed his hands. I was rather peeved
by his ingenuous enthusiasm. It seemed
that he was revealing his inexperience too
much to his superior, who already had a
good idea of it. I decided to make a different
tone.

"I don't quite see how all this is going to help
you," I said. "You know Fairfax's real name.
And you know where he went from to Hammersmith over two years ago. But you don't know
where he is now. Or, in fact," I added ironically,
"if he is now."

"That's true," said Stute, quite unruffled,
"but you expect too much at a time, Townsend.
As I'm always telling you, detection is not done
by leaps and bounds. Now we want to trace

this Fairfax, or Ferris, or Freeman, and his wife.
If he is alive, he will certainly be able to tell us
a good deal and perhaps everything we want to
know. And if he's dead, then his wife will.
Either way, it is worth our while to find out all
we can of him in his pre-Hammersmith days,
and by that means we may be able to find out
where to look for him, or his wife, or his widow,
now."

"So you're going to Long Highbury?"

"I am. Would you like to come?"

I hesitated. Really, to drive all the way to
Oxfordshire on the chance that someone in a
certain village remembered a man who had been
there, perhaps for only a short time, over two
years ago, seemed a little over-optimistic to me.
Besides, even if they did remember him, what
could they say that would help Stute now?
Surely this Fairfax was not the man to spread
the story of his life among his casual acquaintances in the village, and even less his plans for
the future. Still, it was kind of Stute to suggest
my going with him, and it would have been
churlish to refuse. So I accepted with as much
enthusiasm as I could manage.

"You won't need me, sir," questioned Beef.

"No, I don't think so, Sergeant." Then, as
though to conciliate him, Stute added, "We
must keep someone on the spot."

Beef nodded solemnly. "Just so, sir. Any
partic'lar line of enquiry you'd wish me to
follow?"

Stute gave his rather cynical smile. "Nothing
I can think of," he said, "but perhaps

you'll get some interesting information from Mr. Simmons or Mr. Sawyer, while I'm away."

Beef did not see that the detective was pulling his leg. "I'll do my best, sir," he said, and left us.

"You'd better pack a bag, Townsend," Stute said to me. "It's about sixty miles away, and if we don't get our information straight away we may have to stay the night."

"Oh, very well. But doesn't it seem. . . ."

"A long shot? I don't think so. After all, Fairfax is our favourite for the murder stakes at the moment, isn't he? Anything we can find out will help. Our people are working in London to try to trace some associates of his there—but that's a different proposition. They can go among the known drug people, and they'll be met with blank faces. But in a village this size he must have talked to someone."

"Yes," I said, still dubious. "All right, I'll go and pack a bag."

"I'll pick you up at the Mitre in half an hour, then."

But before I reached the door, Constable Galsworthy entered.

"Well?" snapped Stute, who had never forgiven the athletic Galsworthy for his name, which Stute seemed to consider pretentious.

"Got something to report, sir."

"What about?"

"The case, sir."

"The case? What is it?"

"I've been making enquiries. . . ."

"*You*'ve been making enquiries! By whose orders?"

Galsworthy remained admirably calm, and my sympathies were wholly with him. Stute, I thought, was being altogether too discouraging.

"On my own initiative, sir."

"I see. Were you at a public school?"

"Yes, sir."

"I knew it! The Force is full of you fellows. Every constable in England begins to think he's a detective nowadays. Well, what have your enquiries told you?"

"I went to the railway station, sir," said Galsworthy, apparently quite oblivious of Stute's hostility, "and enquired there of the staff whether any of them had seen Fairfax leave for London on the Wednesday of the suicide, sir. It occurred to me that we had their statements with regard to Rogers and Smythe, but no enquiry had been made about Fairfax."

"And you thought it your business to make it?"

"Yes, sir." Still he was quite unimpassioned. "It appears that Fairfax travelled up to London that day on the 2.50."

"I see. And from what does it appear that he travelled up to London?"

"He bought his ticket, sir, and mentioned to the booking-clerk that his little holiday was over. He then spoke to one of the porters on the platform, who saw him into the train. It was a slow train, and only one other passenger was travelling. The porter saw that he went."

"I see. And in the innocence of your Old Etonian heart. . . ."

"Old Berkhampsteadian, sir."

"Don't interrupt. I don't care if it's Old Giggleswickian. In the innocence of your heart you suppose that the fact that a man buys a ticket and gets on a London-bound train, which stops at a dozen intermediate stations, constitutes proof that he travelled to London."

"Not proof, sir."

"No. Do I understand that you have entered for the Police Boxing Championship?"

"Yes, sir."

"I hope you get knocked out. That will do."

Still perfectly calm, Galsworthy said, "Thank you, sir," and withdrew.

"Really!" said Stute.

"You seemed a bit hard on him," I said. "He was doing his best."

"I daresay. But one really can't have that sort of thing. Beef's bad enough, with his 'theories.'"

"But after all," I pointed out gently, "you say you want relevant facts. And he certainly gave you one."

Stute turned to me with his rather pleasant if bitter smile. "All right, let's leave it at that," he said. "This case is beginning to fray my nerves. Ridiculous, when you come to think of it, that we can't trace a simple murder. You go and pack your bag. We'll get hold of Mrs. Fairfax, anyway."

And so, half an hour later, I found myself

speeding away from Braxham with a grim and serious Detective Stute, who seemed more rigidly concentrated than ever. Perhaps Constable Galsworthy had unconsciously keyed him up to the pursuit.

CHAPTER XVIII

"Post office first, then Rectory," said Stute, as we approached Long Highbury. "From pretty considerable experience I know them, in nine cases out of ten, to be the main gossip-shops. Pubs, postmen, and porters are sometimes useful, but their memories are shorter."

"Well, you should know."

Now that we were actually drawing near to the scene of our enquiries I felt rather more interest in them. The long drive across country had made me sleepy in the early afternoon, but as we flashed by the first outlying houses of the village, built of grey Cotswold stone, for Long Highbury was near the Gloucestershire border, I was fully awake again.

The village itself was most attractive, a huddle of houses and farms lying in the folds of a light mist. There was the church, a blunt square tower with a long nave drawn behind it, there was the inn, a large building, the gaily-painted boards of which made a gallant contrast with the grey stone of the place. And here, as Stute drew up, I saw the combined village shop and post office.

The door tinkled happily as Stute opened it, and we found ourselves with just room to stand among the goods displayed. An oil-stove gave out a dry warmth and a faint odour of paraffin, but stronger than this latter was the friendly smell of oranges, cheese, bacon, biscuits, and firewood which permeates all village general stores and is rather appetizing than otherwise.

The shopkeeper (and postmaster) looked up through the thick lenses of his spectacles and said, "Yes?"

"A large Players, please," said Stute.

While he was being served he came straight to the point.

"I wonder whether you could help me," he said. "I'm looking for a man called Freeman who was here with his wife some years ago."

The shopkeeper looked up. I suddenly perceived that he possessed that irritating quality, extreme caution.

"What about him?" he asked, non-committally.

"I want to trace him, that's all."

"'Fraid I can't help you," said the shopkeeper. "He was only here a short time."

"I know. But any information you can give me about him would be welcome. I'm from Scotland Yard," he added.

Again that wary glance. "What has he done?" asked the shopkeeper.

Stute seemed to think that in order to get what he wanted he must give a certain amount in return.

"It's not what he's done," he returned, "but we have reason to think that he may have been murdered."

The shopkeeper looked suitably startled. "What, round here?" he asked.

"No, no. In quite a different part of the world. At any rate Mr. Freeman is missing, and I hoped you might be able to tell us something about him which would help us to trace him."

At that the shopkeeper really seemed to make an effort to recall Freeman.

"I don't think I can. He had what we call the Old Cottage, at the other end of the village. He was there about six months. Very quiet people, they were. Paid up weekly."

"Know where they came from?"

"No. I understood that they had just retired. They meant to settle down here, but they found it too quiet for them."

"Where did they go to?"

"That I can't say. But I daresay the Rector might be able to tell you. They went to church a good deal, I understood."

"Did they?" asked Stute.

"Oh yes. Great church people. We're chapel ourselves, so of course we know nothing about that. But it's what I heard."

"Did they make any other friends here?" asked Stute.

"Not that I know of. They were quite civil with everyone but not what you'd call sociable. I believe I remember hearing something about Mr. Freeman giving a big subscription to one of the Rector's charities, but I don't know what truth there was in that."

"I'm very much obliged to you," said Stute, "and I'll see the Rector. Good afternoon."

I had been amused to notice, during this

interview, what a different manner of question-ing Stute had when he was dealing with a person from whom information had to be drawn. When people came up to him breath-less with excitement and anxious to tell all they knew, he was curt and chilly. But with a man like this he could be polite, almost insinuating.

"That's something new about our friend Fairfax," he said, "A church-goer, was he? Well, well. Some of our neatest criminals have been that."

We got back into the car, and Stute asked a passing errand boy the way to the Rectory. He pointed towards a great grey-stone house, half visible from where we sat, and some three hundred yards away. It stood among splendid trees, but it had that look of slightly decayed grandeur which so many of such parsonages, built towards the beginning of the last century, seem to have nowadays. The gate into the drive was open, and we soon pulled up before an imposing porch.

Stute tugged at a wrought-iron bell-pull, and somewhere in the bowels of the house a bell tolled lugubriously. After an interval a diminutive servant appeared.

"Is the Rector in?" asked Stute.

"What name?" piped the child.

"Inspector Stute and Mr. Townsend."

The servant looked rather startled, and hesitated.

"It's all right," smiled Stute. "We have only come to make a few enquiries."

As though hypnotized, the small servant backed into the hall, and we followed her. She showed us, without speaking, into a draughty drawing-room without a fire in it, and disappeared. I glanced about me at the crowded but chilly display of ornamental china, and shuddered.

But the Rector soon entered, and to our relief we found that he had none of the rowdy egotism of the Vicar of Chopley. He was a little lean, rather unwashed-looking man, with half an inch of underclothing showing below his cuff at either wrist. But he had a conciliatory smile, and a manner of speaking at once jerky and ingratiating.

"I understand," he said, "that you represent Scotland Yard. Wish to ask me some questions?"

"That's so," said Stute. "I want to ask you about a man called Freeman."

"Freeman? Do you mean my Curate? Really, how very disagreeable. Has he been guilty of some misdemeanour? I have always refused to listen to the rumours there have been. . . ."

"No, no," said Stute, impatiently.

I was reminded of Beef's reflections that morning. You never know what you're going to find out about anyone he said. But I made no remark.

"No, sir," Stute went on, "not your curate. A man called Freeman and his wife who lived here about two years and three months ago. He occupied, I understand, the Old Cottage in your parish."

The Rector smiled nervously. "Oh you mean

Mr. Hugo Freeman. Why yes, to be sure. Charming people. But surely. . . ." he suddenly grew serious.

"The supposition is," explained Stute, "that this man Freeman may have been murdered."

"Murdered, eh? Dear, dear. Well I never. That's bad. Delightful people, too. Look here, we can't stand talking here. Come along into the study. We were just going to have tea. My wife will be most interested. That is, distressed. Come along. Give me your coats. Poor Freeman. Well, well. In the midst of life. This way, please."

He led us through the tiled hall, and opened a door beyond it. I was delighted at the prospect of a cup of tea, and gladly entered the study.

If the drawing-room had been cold, this was in distinct contrast. I can only describe it as stuffy. It was a small room, over-furnished, and a bright fire lit its grate. I could see no less than three cats, and had reason to suppose that there were more. In an arm-chair by the fire the Rector's wife was sitting and replaced a piece of buttered crumpet on her plate before greeting us. She was a big blowsy woman with untidy hair, and a voice like a man's.

"My dear," began the Rector, "from Scotland Yard. Inspector Stute. Mr. Townsend. It's about poor Freeman."

The Rector's wife sat up, too startled to acknowledge the informal introduction. "You know what I always told you," she said loudly. "You ought never to have given him so much liberty. . . ."

"No, no, my dear. Not Freeman. Hugo Freeman. At the Old Cottage, you remember. Poor fellow. It appears he's been murdered."

"Oh," said his wife, evidently relieved, "I thought you meant Freeman. Do sit down, Inspector. I'll ring for some fresh tea. Murdered, you say? (Get down, will you, Tibbits. You shall have your milk presently.) How very, very terrible. They were *such* nice people."

Stute, gratefully eating bread and butter, seemed content to let the talk take its own course.

The Rector went on. "Yes, charming folk. Just retired, so I understood. Business for many years in Liverpool. Accountancy, I believe. Most wearing. I'm no good at figures. And they hoped to settle here. Pity, now, they didn't. Such a quiet parish. But plenty to do," he added, hurriedly, "plenty to do."

"My husband works much too hard. I always tell him he's too conscientious. He'll wear himself out. But about Mr. Freeman. I wonder who could have murdered him. Ah, here's your tea. Two lumps. And you, Mr. Townsend? So you're investigating the case, Inspector?"

"Well, it's not quite as simple as that. We don't know that Freeman has been murdered. But he's disappeared."

"There, there. Poor fellow," said the Rector. "Such a good chap. So generous. Only had to ask him. Do anything for the church. How was he murdered? Oh, you don't know of course. Try that cake, do."

"I was wondering," managed Stute, "whether you could help us."

"Delighted," murmured the Rector mechanically, "anything I can do."

"Do you know where he had come from when he got here?"

"Where was it, my dear? Liverpool, wasn't it? Or Birmingham?"

"Manchester, I rather think," said his wife.

"One of those places, anyway," summarized the Rector.

"And what did you say had been his profession?"

"He had just retired when he got here. Accountancy. Estate Agent. Something of the sort. I forget the details. But he had substantial means."

"Quite. And while he was here?"

"Exemplary. A splendid parishioner. Regularly at church. Helping hand. A charming man."

"And after he had gone?"

"We never heard from them. Most disappointing. But people are like that. My wife was hurt at first."

"Well, it was rather rude," said the Rector's wife.

"Didn't you write to them?"

"They forgot to leave their address. And the post office never had it, either. They had to return several letters, I understand. Chiefly circulars, Brown said. Brown's our postmaster. Long-headed chap."

"So you've no idea where the Freemans went?"

"They hadn't decided. They were going to put their furniture into store, they said. Have a holiday. Poor souls, they'd never been abroad."

"You mean they went abroad from here?"

"Yes. To France."

"How did you know they went to France?"

"They told me so. Besides, I signed their application for a passport."

Stute was silent a moment, staring fixedly at the nervous Rector.

"You remember that?" he asked at last.

"Indeed I do. Freeman was smiling over it. A man of his age who had never needed a passport. Poor chap! His passport's for Another Place now. But that one is in order, I'm sure."

"Have some more cake?" said his wife.

"And what countries was it made out for?"

"France. Only France. I remember that. I remarked on it at the time."

"I see. Well, I needn't trouble you further, Rector. Thank you so much for your information."

"And for tea," I put in, trying to cover his brusqueness with a smile.

"Not at all. Delighted. Pleasure," said the Rector, and I believed him. "Sad business," he added.

"Awfully sad," said his wife. "Sure you won't have any more to eat? (Oh, don't scratch, Lucille.) Was his wife murdered too?"

Stute was already leaving the room, so I gave a rather unsatisfactory shake of the head in answer to this parting question, and then followed the Rector and Inspector through the hall. We shook hands briefly with our host, and went down the steep steps of his gloomy house. Stute hurriedly lit a cigarette, and blew lustily from it, as though there was something in his lungs which he wanted entirely to expel.

CHAPTER XIX

WE must have covered about eight miles at a very fair speed before either of us spoke. The evening had darkened and one could see little more than the shining surface of wet tar ahead of us. I had momentarily forgotten our problems as I thought of the dingy little Rector and his wife.

"Do you still think our visit to Long Highbury wasted?" Stute asked suddenly.

"Well, we don't seem much forrader," I returned. "All we know now is that the Freemans went from there to France."

"You are really a splendid foil, Mr. Townsend. I wish you had taken it into your head to describe one of my cases, instead of Beef's."

I thought this rather rude. "Do you know so much more?" I asked.

"I certainly *don't* know that the Freemans went from Long Highbury to France. But I *do* know why they went to Long Highbury. And I've a pretty good idea of how to get hold of them, or of her, now."

"Remarkable, I'm sure," I snapped with sarcastic incredulity. "If you've learnt all that from our interview in that very unventilated room, I congratulate you."

"My dear Townsend, surely you must see for yourself? Here we have a known criminal,

a man engaged in an extremely remunerative
traffic which may bring him at any moment
under arrest. He suddenly, under a new name,
goes down to the country and takes a cottage,
explaining rather vaguely that he is a retired
accountant of sorts. He takes care to make
friends with the Rector, and to support him
rather lavishly in any appeal he may make.
Then he casually decides to go abroad, and gets
the Rector to sign his application for a passport.
What is the inference?"

I shrugged.

"Well, he was arranging what the Americans
call a hideout. He was planning for a rainy
day. When trouble arose he, Ferris or Fairfax,
whom nobody had reason to associate with a
Mr. Freeman who once lived at Long Highbury,
would have a perfectly authentic passport ready
for him. And it was the *only* way he could get
that passport. The office does not, except in
certain cases, confirm details of birth, etc., given
to them. Provided the application is signed by
a responsible person, they issue the passport.
So that our friend spent six months of his life
in preparing for the dangerous moment when
he would want to vanish. And vanish he could,
completely. I have often wondered why more
criminals don't take this simple precaution. It
may be the church-work which puts them off."

"Good Lord! You really think. . . ."

"I am certain of it. Why else did Ferris-
Fairfax-Freeman spend that time in a village
with that sort of parson? Why else? And we
know that he got his passport, and having got

F

it, disappeared leaving no address which quite distressed the Rector and his wife who thought him 'charming.'"

"Clever idea. He must have been a pretty deep sort of blackguard."

"Yes. Or working for one. I'm inclined to agree with our friend in Buenos Aires about a 'big power' behind this somewhere. Our record of Ferris was of a fairly ordinary type of criminal."

"But you said that you had an idea as to where he is now, if he's still alive. What is that?"

"His passport was made out for France, and France only. I imagine his reason for having that was an idea of his, possibly mistaken, that an application for a passport for France only would not be scrutinized as carefully as one for all countries in Europe. Remember that if the Passport Office had taken it into their heads to ask for a birth certificate, he was sunk. Anyway, presuming that he used that passport he has gone to France, and to get any further he would have to apply to a British Consul."

"That's true."

"So that if we apply to the French police, and at the same time notify our consulates in France, there is a good chance of coming up with him. Always, of course, providing that he's still alive."

"You're quite right, of course. How you people cover the loop-holes."

"Just a matter of being a little bit methodical, and not neglecting any chance of gathering

information. You see? That was why I went
to Long Highbury. It was a chance—and it
has come off. Meanwhile, Ferris-Fairfax-Free-
man, if he *is* alive, can have no idea that we
have linked him with Long Highbury. Why
should he? It was a hundred to one against
that woman in the basement noticing what
firm had moved him. Only the invincible
curiosity of people who live in houses that are
divided into flats about the inhabitants of other
strata, happened to come to our rescue. A
little luck, and a lot of care! That's detection."

After that we drove on in silence for a time.
My conscience was pricking me a little in the
matter of Sergeant Beef. After all, it had been
as his friend that I had first been introduced
to the case, and I had neglected him disgrace-
fully. But Stute was more interesting to watch.
His keen, forceful mind, his habit of pigeon-
holing all his information with infinite care,
his unhurried but resolute progress, his swift
trained senses, were so obviously superior to
the ponderous calculations of Beef that I was
beginning to doubt the Sergeant.

However, I said to myself, as we eventually
approached Braxham, perhaps my old friend
may have unearthed some useful information
for Stute during our absence. He would at
least have plodded on with his search.

At the police station Constable Galsworthy
was waiting for us.

"Sergeant Beef asked me to go and fetch him
when you arrived, sir," he told Stute. "I understand he has something to report."

"Where is he?" the Inspector asked, with the asperity he always showed to this constable.

"He told me to tell you, if you should ask, sir, that he would be prosecuting some of the enquiries you had suggested."

"Oh yes," said Stute, unable to repress his grim smile. "All right. I'll wait here."

We sat down and smoked in silence, both of us very tired. It must have been a quarter of an hour later that Beef hurried in, perspiring slightly, but quite pleased with himself.

"Well, Beef?" said Stute at once.

"You're a marvel, sir!" said the Sergeant loudly. "'Ow you can 'ave known I can't make out."

"Known what?" asked Stute rather coldly.

"Why, that I should get that information from Sawyer wot you told me to go for."

Stute nodded. "What is it?"

"Well, 'e didn't want to say nothink at first. But seeing that you'd told me to go an' cross-examine 'im again, I knew there must be some-think 'e could tell. Besides, I could see in 'is eye 'e was 'iding it. So I kep' on at 'im. And after a lot of questioning 'e outs with it."

"What?" asked Stute impatiently.

"Why about 'is brother, sir."

"His brother? Sawyer's brother? What about him?"

"Don't you know, sir? I thought you must 'ave to 'ave sent me down there. Why, 'e's disappeared. Clean vanished."

Stute groaned. "Not another murderee!" he begged.

"I'll tell you wot 'e told me. This 'ere brother of 'is is married. And when I say married— well, she's a reg'lar Tartar. You know, takes 'is wages orf 'im an' all that. If 'e so much as goes near a pub she's arfter 'im. I've seen 'er myself when she's been over 'ere with 'im at the Dragon. Really narsty she gets."

Stute sighed. "They didn't live here?" he asked wearily.

"No, sir. Ower at Claydown."

"How far away is that?"

"It'd be about fifteen miles. It's the best shopping centre round here. Sawyer's brother was a painter and decorator with a little business of 'is own. 'E'd of got on nicely if it 'adn't been for that wife of 'is."

Stute's eyes were closed, but Beef wasn't to be hurried.

"On that Wednesday 'e came in to the Dragon. . . ."

"Time?" said Stute.

"I was coming to that. Round about seven o'clock. Not long after young Rogers 'ad gone out. And he calls 'is brother aside. 'Fred,' 'e says, 'I've run away.' 'Run away?' says Sawyer. 'Yes,' 'e says, 'from 'er.' 'Good Lord!' says Sawyer, not 'ardly blaming 'im, you understand, but took aback all the same. 'What you going ter do?' 'e asks. 'Well,' says 'is brother, 'she's got the business. She'll keep the two men on and do just as well as if I was there.' Sawyer said 'e could quite believe that. But what 'is brother wanted was for 'im to lend 'im some money. See, she wrote all the cheques an' that. 'E couldn't draw nothink without 'er. See?"

"And did he?" sighed Stute.

"Yes. Ten quid 'e lent 'im. And 'is brother promised to write to 'im. 'E'd left a note for 'is wife, saying 'e couldn't stick the sight of 'er no more."

"That wasn't very polite," remarked Stute.

"Well, if you'd of seen 'er, sir! Anyway, off 'e goes."

"What time?"

"Sawyer couldn't say for certain, but it must of been about an hour after 'e come in."

"I see. Well, what do you expect me to do about it?"

Beef seemed taken aback. "You arst me to find out from Sawyer. . . ."

Stute stood up. "All right, Sergeant. I'm sure you did your best. But I really don't see why you should expect me to be interested in Mr. Sawyer's lost brother. I don't suppose he even *knew* young Rogers?"

"A certain amount, 'e did, anyway."

"Still, even knowing him scarcely seems a reason to be murdered, does it?"

Beef looked sulky. "Well, there you are. I done what you said. And I told you the result."

"Thank you, Beef," said Stute, icily. And the meeting was adjourned.

CHAPTER XX

DAYS passed again without further revelations. At this point I really began to wonder whether it ever would be discovered whom Rogers had murdered. If Beef's story of Sawyer's brother was to be taken seriously there were now four possibilities. The whole thing was nightmarish, and I was reminded of the time when, a frightened preparatory schoolboy, I used to wake up and find myself trying to work out on my pillow the mathematical problems set in class.

The worst of the case was that nothing seemed absolutely certain. There were probabilities, possibilities, theories, but nothing that one could get hold of.

And then one morning came an event which eliminated one of the possibilities, and at the same time gave new hope of a solution. It was a windy clear day in March, and there were snow-drops in the Braxham gardens, and the first indications of Spring, I remember. And Beef, instead of looking dull and liverish, seemed jovial that morning, and gave a twirl to his moustache instead of sucking it peevishly.

"They've found 'im," he said excitedly. "This 'ere Fairfax."

"You mean . . . his body? It *was* Fairfax?"

"No!" Beef's negative was drawn through a

series of vowels. "Alive an' kicking. Very much alive, I should think. 'E's in Paris."

Stute, less emotionally, confirmed the news.

"He went to our consulate in Paris," he said. "It appears that he wanted to move on to Switzerland. We have his address in Paris, and the French police are watching him in the meanwhile. His wife is with him."

"What will you do next?"

"Run across," said Stute. "I'm taking Beef with me."

"Taking me?" gasped Beef. "Wotever for?"

"You know the man. I never trust a photo for identification. I want someone with me who knows him by sight."

"Gor! 'N've I gotter goter France?"

"You'd better be ready in half an hour. We must catch the mid-day boat."

Beef didn't seem able to take it in. "I don't know wot my wife'll say. Me going to Paris. I 'aven't been over since the War."

"Well, you're going now. Hurry up and change."

Beef blundered out of the room as though he were dazed.

"Only way," explained Stute sharply, as though he were trying to convince himself as well as me. "Must have someone who knows the fellow."

I was, let me confess, wondering whether I should join them. I had been in Braxham just three weeks now, and had seen this case from the beginning. There were no claims on my time, and it really seemed that having stayed through all these preliminary routine enquiries I ought to follow the thing through to its climax. Besides, there was an element of the grotesque about this proposed expedition which appealed to me. Beef in Paris! The idea was enticing. And Fairfax, after all, was the person whose information would be most likely to be both surprising and useful.

"Would you mind if I came?" I asked Stute.

"Funny chap you are. You weren't anxious to come to Long Highbury because you didn't think it would produce anything. Yet for this, which is far more likely to be a wild goose chase, you're keen. Come if you like, by all means. Only don't be disappointed if it turns out not to be our Fairfax at all. Or if he won't speak. Or if his information, after all, is valueless. I shouldn't be surprised, you know."

"I won't be disappointed," I promised.

"But how can you spare the time to follow us round? Don't you ever *do* anything?"

"I write detective novels," I admitted.

Stute made a curious and I thought rather hostile sound with his lips.

But soon we were tearing across country to catch the mid-day boat. There was a pale blue sky and sunlight which, at least after the winter months, seemed quite warm. And at last we were going somewhere, doing something. I felt really happy.

Beef seemed to feel the same. "This ain't 'arf a lark," he said, "is it? I mean, 'ere we are off to Paris. It don't seem possible."

Stute made no reply, apparently concentrating on the road.

"You think, then, Sergeant, that the information we shall get from Fairfax'll clear things up, do you?"

"I never said nothink about that," returned Beef guardedly, "that's for Inspector Stute to say. But I mean, it's an outing, i'n't it?"

It certainly was. With Beef in the most police-like clothes I have ever seen, with even a pair of large boots to conform to precedent, and Stute, as ever, quietly dressed and inconspicuously refined, we made a queer trio.

"Good sailor, Sergeant?" I asked Beef presently, since Stute seemed disinclined to talk.

"Well, I've only done it during the War," said Beef, "and then—well, you know what it was."

I could well imagine, and said no more. But as soon as we were on the usual Cross-Channel steamer and out at sea, it was quite obvious that Beef was not a good sailor. His crimson face turned a curious mauvish tint, and he made no further attempt to be talkative.

"I don't 'arf feel queer," he admitted later; and quite suddenly left us.

Stute had not time to notice the contretemps. His mind was busy with our chances. He told me, frowning, that he believed the fellow Fairfax would talk, at any rate on the drug issue. But what he, Stute, had to do was to find out by carefully-framed questions whether Fairfax had any hand in the murder.

"There's just one other chance," said Stute.

"This fellow we're going to see may not be Fairfax. We know he's got the passport that was issued in the name of Freeman. But a Foreign Office stamp over the photograph can be faked easily enough. Suppose that Fairfax is dead. . . ."

Just then Beef joined us again, looking much better.

"Wonderful wot a drop of brandy'll do for you," he said.

But after that Stute kept his speculations to himself.

I was delighted when our train steamed into Paris at last, and felt quite important when two very stern and preoccupied men came up to Stute. There were introductions and enquiries about the smoothness or otherwise of the passage, but no smiles.

All five of us got into a smart police car which fought its way out of the station traffic most admirably. Beef was staring about him with wonder in his round eyes. He was sitting next to me, and made little remarks in my ear continually. He hadn't heard this language since the War, he said. It made you feel "funny" to hear it again. He wouldn't like to live in a country where darts was not played. And it would be awkward to be a policeman if you had to wear the uniform used here. He didn't know what they'd say in Braxham if he turned out like that.

I tried to discourage his commentary for I was anxious to hear the more serious matters under discussion between his superiors.

"What seems most odd," one of the French detectives was saying in excellent English, "is his complete confidence. He does not seem to consider the possibility of his being followed."

Stute smiled. "He is a clever man, or has a clever man behind him. But for a piece of luck he never would have been followed." And Stute told them in outline of Fairfax's scheme, and how he had gone to the trouble and expense of building up a new identity in the village of Long Highbury for the sole object of getting a passport under another name ready for an emergency.

The Frenchmen were impressed. "Neat," they admitted, "but you were thorough. That is how you get your men over there—thoroughness."

"Method. Order," murmured Stute mechanically.

"Well, we are having him watched, your friend. Already you have helped us not a little. He has been to a lady's beauty parlour which we have long suspected of selling drugs. But we are making no investigation there until you have seen your man. We did not wish to scare him away."

"Good. Very considerate of you. Looks as though this case is going to mean quite a round-up of the drugs crowd."

"What can we want better? Their arrest is always a credit to the police."

"'Ere!" said Sergeant Beef with a sudden explosiveness across me, "'ave you got any ideas as to 'oo they mean by the big shot in this drugs game. I see those South American chaps thought there was someone be'ind it all."

"No," said the French detective rather coldly, "we have not."

Stute seemed to think that he was called upon to explain away Beef's outburst.

"The Sergeant," he said in his passionless voice, "is coming with me to identify Fairfax. He knew the man by sight, and I didn't. The Sergeant is not at Scotland Yard."

"Understood," said one of the Frenchmen.

"Perfectly," nodded the other.

"All the same," said Beef pensively, "it wouldn't 'arf be a good thing to find out."

We had passed the statue of Balzac, and seemed to be making for Passy.

"Now, I hope you understand the position so far as we're concerned," said one of the Frenchmen to Stute. "We have found your man, and we have watched him for you. But we have no reason at present to make an arrest, and there is, of course, no question of extradition for the moment. He is staying with his wife in a highly respectable hotel. We have seen the proprietor, and promised him that there will be no scene or scandal. He will be helpful so far as he can, but he is naturally anxious to protect his other guests from any annoyance. So that all you can do is to interview the man and his wife."

"That's all I want to do."

"Good. And if in your interview you fail to get what you want then we will proceed with our investigation at the beauty parlour, and should we get evidence there against this man

Fairfax, or Freeman, or Ferris, as he variously calls himself, we will arrest him, and hope that you complete your case in England while we hold him. Right?"

"Splendid," said Stute.

"I have read the whole case," put in the other detective, "I think it was the girl that he murdered. I think that this drug business is interesting, but irrelevant to the main crime."

"Indeed?" snapped Stute, "you are no doubt better able to follow it from this distance."

The French detective explained quickly that he had wished to imply nothing of the sort. He was merely theorizing.

"I have never," said Stute, "known a case which gave such scope for theorizing. It is facts that I want. And if I can't get some out of Fairfax I shall begin to be annoyed. This investigation has gone on long enough."

"We are nearly there. The proprietor will be expecting us."

"Good," said Stute. "Are their rooms in the front of the house?"

"No. At the back. I asked particularly, having regard to our arrival."

We drew up at a quiet-looking house in the rue Vineuse, with only a small plate to indicate that it was a hotel. Everything about it was neat, discreet, smart. It was the sort of place, I judged, which charged high prices, but gave value for them. No one was in sight as our taxi stopped, and we three got out. One of the two Frenchmen turned quickly to Stute.

"We will await you at the corner," he said, "Good luck."

The car moved quietly away and our incongruous trio advanced towards the front door.

CHAPTER XXI

THE hotel-proprietor, who was as neat and discreet as the exterior of his hotel, was waiting for us in the entrance.

"It is room Number 39 that you want," he said. "I have just sent cocktails up, so I think you arrive at a good moment. And please, no disturbance."

His voice had dropped almost to a whisper, and he had nervously pulled a scented handkerchief from the pocket of his black jacket. He eyed Beef somewhat dubiously, but it was Stute who answered him.

"We only want a little talk," he said flatly.

There was a small slow lift, and we crossed to it, but found that we were only just able to get in, for the proprietor accompanied us. On the second floor we stepped out, and the proprietor led the way down a thickly carpeted passage. At Room 39 he stopped and motioning us near, tapped sharply.

"Yes?" replied a masculine voice, then added impatiently, "Come in."

"Some gentlemen to see you," said the proprietor, and before there was time for a move from the inside, he flung open the door. Instantly, we pushed in.

It was a sitting-room, evidently the outer apartment of a suite. In two arm-chairs, both, as it happened, facing or half-facing the door, were a man and woman staring up at us in astonishment. The man was dressed in English tweeds, but his heavy-jowled face was pasty and pouchy. At first, looking at that couple, one might have thought them a middle-aged English tourist and his wife, normal, nice, provincial people. But somehow there was something wrong. I could not define it then, I cannot now, but I was aware that something unpleasant distinguished this couple from the type they so nearly resembled. Stute turned quickly to Beef, and whispered "Fairfax?"

The Sergeant nodded, thereby fulfilling his whole purpose in our visit to France.

When the man spoke, his voice had that curious closed ring in it which is noticeable in people who form their speech too far back in their throat.

"What's this?" he said.

"Sorry to disturb you, Mr. Freeman. But I would like to ask you a few questions. I'm Detective-Inspector Stute."

"But. . . ."

"Yes. You're quite right. This is Sergeant Beef of Braxham. An unfortunate combination from your point of view, Mr. Fairfax. But there you are."

"I don't know. . . ."

"No, of course you don't yet, Mr. Ferris. We all have a lot to explain to one another. And as none of us want to waste time perhaps it would be best if I told you first what *we* know. Then you won't have to waste time giving us a lot

of unnecessary information. In the first place
we know that your real name is Ferris, and that
you have done time for drug-peddling. In the
second place we know that you are identical
with that much more respectable Mr. Hugo
Freeman who lived for a time in Long Highbury,
and thus got a passport ready for any emergency.
And thirdly we know that you are also that
piscatorial Mr. Fairfax who used to stay at the
Riverside Hotel, Braxham. We also know that
you were receiving drugs from young Rogers.
But there is quite a lot which we don't know,
and which you are going to tell us."

I watched the pair of them. The man had
sunk back in his chair and turned a little pale,
but was not showing any sign of panic or defiance.
He was, I thought, considering, fairly collectedly,
just how to treat all this.

The woman deliberately sipped her cocktail.
She had a raw hard face, with a large mouth and
wide nostrils. She was quite unshaken.

There was a long silence. At last Stute continued.

"To come direct to the point, I will ask you
straight away, who was killed by you and Rogers
that Wednesday night?"

Fairfax seemed relieved at the question. "Look
here," he said, "what are you really after?
Drugs or murder?"

They were almost his first words, and I
respected his perception and decision. He did
not waste time with a lot of stupid bluff. He did
not deny his triple identity. He knew that
Stute was not bluffing, on that point, anyway.

"Both," said Stute.

"Then I can't help you."

"No?"

"No."

Another long silence.

"But I'll tell you this much," said Fairfax at last. "The first I knew of any murder was when I read it in the papers. When I left Braxham to the best of my knowledge young Rogers had no more idea of murdering anyone than I had."

That, I felt, was true.

"What time did you leave Braxham?"

"On the 2.50."

"How far did you go?"

"What d'you mean? Oh, I see. Why, to London, of course."

"Got an alibi?"

Fairfax didn't like that word. "It's got as far as alibis, has it?" he said. "Why should I need an alibi? Who has been murdered, anyway?"

Stute spoke slowly. "I think if you've got an alibi, Ferris, you'd better give it to me."

At this point the woman broke in.

"Do for goodness' sake sit down, Inspector. You give me the jitters standing up all the time. And your . . . staff," she added, with an unfriendly glance at Beef and me.

Stute, without hesitation, accepted, and we followed.

"You'd better have a cocktail," she went on. "Oh, I can assure you it won't be drugged."

"No, thanks. And now, Mr. Ferris."

"Well, if I had known that it would be necessary, I would have arranged an alibi after your own heart for you. As it is, I'm afraid it may be rather sketchy. I had a hair-cut first, in the station saloon."

Stute never took written notes. Information was stored more securely in his head.

"Then," said Ferris, "since I had left all our small luggage at Braxham, I went and bought two handbags at a shop called Flexus, in the Strand. I had them sent to our address in Hammersmith, so that the shop will probably have a record of my call. I then had a drink, since it was just opening time, at the Sword on the Cross in Fragrant Street, Covent Garden. I think the bar-maid might remember my call as there was a little altercation with an itinerant vendor of a publication called the *War-Cry* while I was in the bar."

"Yes?"

"I had a meal in the Brasserie of Lyons Corner House in Coventry Street. I sat, I well remember, at a table near the orchestra, and was attended by a tall young waiter. After that I went to the Flintshire Hotel, just off Russell Square, where I booked a room for the night."

"In your own name?"

"Er, not actually. I can't think why not. Habit I suppose. Fortescue was the name I chose."

"Well, go on."

"I did. I went out and had two drinks at a strange pub whose name I don't remember, and returned soon after ten, to bed. I had occasion, not long afterwards, to tap on the wall, and admonish a lady and gentleman involved in a somewhat stormy argument."

"I see. If that all checks up, you seem to be fairly well accounted for. Why didn't you go home that night?"

"Really, Inspector, what a question. Surely you can use your powers of deduction better than that."

"Oh, tell him, Sam," said his wife suddenly. "You're not admitting anything now. We don't want this murder business pestering us."

Fairfax considered. "Perhaps you're right," he said. "Well, let's put it this way, Inspector. Suppose—mind you I only suppose—that there had been certain dealing as between young Rogers and me, which I wasn't anxious to have scrutinized. And suppose that that afternoon, while I was with young Rogers in the Dragon, we had observed a gentleman whom we thought anxious *to* scrutinize them. . . ."

"The foreigner!" I couldn't help putting in.

"And suppose that therefore I decided to . . . go away for a holiday, as it were, as promptly as practicable. Well, you see? I might not think my home address the healthiest of all places in London. I might not have wished either to return to the pretentious precincts of Riverside Private Hotel, or to my flat in Hammersmith just then."

"You mean, you thought the foreigner was a policeman? That he had followed young Rogers from Buenos Aires?"

"Well, he had been on the boat."

"I see. So you telephoned your wife, and the two of you used the passport you had ready. Very opportune."

Stute was thoughtful.

"Why didn't you want Rogers to go back to Buenos Aires?" he asked.

"*That* didn't sound healthy either. With a gentleman following him from there. He might have been asked awkward questions in Buenos Aires. And not in the gentle and courteous way you have here."

"Mm. How long had you known Rogers?"

"About two years."

"And your bi-monthly visits to Braxham, 'for the fishing,' coincided with his leave every time, and were made solely with the object of collecting the dope he brought over."

"Now you're becoming personal, Inspector."

"I'm not going to ask you where he got it, how much he brought, or for whom you were working. I know such questions would be useless. But I think you have the sense to see that if you had nothing to do with the murder young Rogers did, you had best tell me anything you know. We could very soon extradite you on the other charge if we thought you were keeping anything back."

"I have seen your point since we began talking," said Fairfax. "What do you want to know?"

"Have you any reason to suppose that Rogers might later have attacked that foreigner?"

"Well, you never know what a man's nerves will make him do when he's being followed. But he had absolutely no thought of it when I left him. He was full of a girl he was to meet that evening."

"And that afternoon?"

"He had an appointment in Chopley. He didn't tell me what it was."

"When did you see him last?"

"After we came out of the Mitre we walked towards the station and Riverside. At the entrance to the station I left him, and he was going on to pick up his motor-bike which he had left in the Riverside drive."

Every point in the man's story seemed to me to accord perfectly with our information. He had evidently been engaged in drug-smuggling, but was hoping that he might escape extradition on this charge while the graver affair overshadowed it.

"Incidentally, Inspector, I have retired."

"Retired?"

"Exactly. We needn't explain from what. I am not a criminal. I am a human being who wanted money, a lot of money, very badly. And I've got it. Quite securely, thank you. And now my wife and I are going to turn our energies to quite other matters. I have always been a keen antiquarian. Research is to be our future."

"*Now* won't you have a cocktail?" said Mrs. Fairfax.

"No, thanks. Well, before you do any research, you're going to do another stretch, Ferris. Here, in France, my friend. The French police have been following you, and know your relations with that beauty parlour."

Ferris smiled. "Not a bit of it," he said. "My call was purely cautionary. I have never done anything in this country for which I could be blamed by even the mildest curé. No, such days are over. We always meant to retire to France when the time came. And the appearance of that foreign gentleman in Braxham meant that the time had come. There is no charge whatever that can be brought against me in France, and I don't quite see how you're going to formulate one in England."

"Wot about your passport?" asked Beef suddenly. "It's a wrong 'un. The French'll send you back over that, and then you'll be for it in England."

"I think not," said Ferris. "I have my own legitimate passport of course, though I didn't think it wise to use it yet, imagining in the innocence of my heart that if anyone was pursued here it would be Ferris; not Freeman. However, now that we've had this little chat, I must use my own."

I will own that we stared at him, even Stute stared at him, with something like wonder. He was no ordinary blackguard.

Then Stute stood up smartly. "Your 'retirement' as you call it, depends on a number of things. In the first place on the truth of your statements about Braxham, and your alibi. In the second, on whether or not we extradite you for drug-peddling in England. In the third, on whether you're speaking the truth about your innocence in France."

"Quite," said Fairfax in his cool and even

voice, "But I don't think that you and I are going to meet again, Inspector."

"In any case, you'll be watched while I'm finishing my investigations in England."

"Then I do hope you'll be quick. My wife has never been to see the winter sports, and I've promised her a stay this year."

CHAPTER XXII

THE return was less cheerful than the voyage out. It seemed that we had got what evidence Fairfax could supply, and that so far from being helpful it set us back. That was the maddening thing about the case—the more of it that was cleared up, the further receded the solution. Stute had begged for facts, and had promised to form a full explanation from them. But the more he learnt the less he knew.

"Do you believe Fairfax's story?" I asked, when we were on board our home-bound channel steamer.

"Yes. I'm afraid I do. We shall check his details, of course, and see if we can follow a few more of his movements as a drug-vendor. But I'm pretty certain that they will be incidental to the main issue. I don't think he was directly concerned in the murder. I shouldn't be surprised, in fact, if he's speaking the truth when he says that his first knowledge of it came from reading the newspaper."

"Strange type."

"Yes. Not at all usual. It is so rarely that a criminal looks ahead. I should think he owes that much to the wife. But I should like to get evidence against him. He was clever enough and imaginative enough all the time he was selling cocaine to know at whose expense he was getting rich. Wretched little addicts who were throwing away their lives. Whatever is right or wrong it is pretty certain that giving people narcotics is a moral crime as well as a legal one."

I was anxious to return to the problem, and to know what Stute would make of it now. One of the possibilities had been, provisionally, removed. To which of the others would he turn?

"What line are you going on now?" I asked, taking advantage of the fact that he liked thinking aloud to me.

"I suppose," he said, "I shall come back to the girl. There is not yet the remotest evidence that Rogers even met the foreigner. Whereas we have actually got a motive when it comes to Smythe. And in this hotch-potch, a motive alone is worth worrying over."

"But I thought you ruled the girl out. You explained to me why it could not very well have been her."

"I know, I know," snapped Stute irritably, "but what the devil is one to go on in this preposterous case. Where's Beef?"

"He said he was going to lie down. He doesn't feel his best as sea."

Stute continued to talk peevishly.

"I've had enough of this investigation," he said. "And they'll be getting impatient at the Yard soon."

"You can always report that there *was* no murder," I suggested.

"I wish I could. But then—why did the fellow commit suicide? A man of Rogers's stamp doesn't swallow cyanide of potassium for nothing. And if there wasn't a murder there was violence, and I can't even find that. No, there's no way out. I've got three chances. Fairfax's alibi may be a dud, so that I can prove that he was involved. I may be able to see a way out of the impasse I reached in the possibility of its being the girl. Or something may come to light about the foreigner."

"You don't think there can be anything in Beef's story of Sawyer's brother?"

Stute shrugged. "There might be," he said, "but if we've got to trace every husband who is escaping an insufferable wife just now, we might as well call in every policeman in Great Britain. However, I can keep it as a last resource. And now," he turned to me quite politely, but with some of that terseness I had noticed him show to others, "would you mind leaving me to think this out?"

I obediently went in search of Beef, and found him moaning at the bar, with a whisky and soda in his hand.

"I *do* feel bad," he said. "I 'ope I never 'ave a case wot takes me abroad again. Don't you feel at all queer?"

"Not at all," I assured him. "It's quite smooth."

"Smoove you call it? I call it 'orrible."

"Stute doesn't seem too cheerful," I said to reassure him, "but it's not seasickness with him. He's worried about this case."

"Wonderful man," said Beef. "'E doesn't miss nothink. Look at the way 'e notices every

detail. Thorough, that's wot 'e is. I shouldn't
'ave seen 'arf of wot 'e 'as. Still, that's training."

"Bit different from the amateurs?" I suggested,
glad that Beef was realizing his own limitations.

"Different thing altogether. 'E 'asn't got a
lot of these 'ere theories like wot they went on.
He 'as facts, and works from that."

"Have you got any solution, Beef?" I asked
narrowly.

Beef turned to the barman. "I'll 'ave another
whisky," he said.

"Have you?" I repeated sternly, watching
his crimson face.

"Well," he admitted, "I 'ave got wot might
be the beginnings of an idea. Only it wouldn't
do for me to say nothink yet. Besides, I think
'e's on to it now, or *part* of it anyway. So don't
you go an' open your mouth."

"I won't. But I think you might tell me."

"It 'asn't gone far enough to say a word at
present," returned Beef.

But we were interrupted. Stute hurried down
and stood between us. There was more vivacity
in his passionless face than I had ever seen.

"Come on deck," he said, presumably to
both of us, but more to me than to Beef, "I've
got something to tell you."

We followed him on to the deck, but no sooner
had we started to pace it than Beef excused
himself hurriedly again, and went below.

"I believe I've got it," Stute said. "I'm not
sure, but you may as well hear what I think."

I nodded, and reflected that Stute had become
a much more human person recently.

"You remember when we were considering the girl Smythe," he said, "we were up against what seemed an insuperable barrier. He had no time to murder her after being seen with her by Meadows, and before being seen without her in the pub by Sawyer. Or if he *had* time, he had no place. We dismissed the chance of the person in the white mackintosh being someone else impersonating Smythe, and we thought it most unlikely that she had been obliging enough to wait in Braxham to be murdered later in the evening. That was, more or less, our case against its having been the girl."

"Well?"

"Suppose, Townsend, suppose he had killed her *before* being seen by Meadows. . . ."

"But. . . ."

"Yes, Meadows saw her all right—behind the headlight of the motor-bike. But did he *hear* her? Did he, in fact, have any reason to suppose that she was alive at that time?"

"My God!" The possibilities which this opened up were positively gruesome.

"Look here, I'll state the case, and you point out the flaws. Young Rogers was a wastrel from the start—we know that. He had this affair with Smythe, wrote the usual breach-of-promise letters, and shook her off. Two years ago he met Fairfax at a local pub and started bringing in cocaine for him from Buenos Aires. During this last leave by a coincidence the two things came to a head—not even a coincidence, really, for troubles never come singly.

The Buenos Aires police had followed him over in the hope of finding out who were his associates *here*, and so tracing them at their end as well. There's nothing improbable in that, they're amazingly thorough, and wouldn't consider the expense. Fairfax realizes that it is all up, tells young Rogers he's finished with it, and advises him not to go back to Buenos Aires. Fairfax leaves young Rogers with this advice, and takes the 2.50 as he claims, while Rogers goes off to see Smythe at Chopley. Either he fails to come to terms with her, or else he pretends to have done so, only stipulating that they must go to Braxham together and get the money from his uncle's house. Perhaps he had already decided to murder her—in which case his purchase of a whole skein of rope was deliberate. Perhaps the rope itself provided the idea. At all events he stopped his motor-bike on the common, and they left it to walk across the grass—as we know from the Vicar of Chopley. It would not have been hard to persuade Smythe into that. He may have pretended a reconciliation. Once hidden from the road he stabs her, takes the letters from her, and burns them then and there, very thoroughly, since he missed only one small segment. Then he sets the dead girl on the pillion of his motor-bike and ties her legs, under her skirt, firmly into place. A piece of rope on to each of her wrists tied in a bow in front of him serves to keep the corpse in place. Or perhaps her wrists were tied to his belt. He drives towards Braxham, but waits on a dark piece of road for someone to come by

through whom he can, if necessary, prove afterwards that Smythe was sitting on the carrier of
his motor-bike at ten to six. It must have been
an anxious time for him, as he daren't wait
later than five to six, because the train, on which
she is supposed to be leaving for London, goes
at six. But along comes Meadows. Perhaps
Rogers knew that he was due to pass. If not it
must have seemed lucky to him. He deliberately
asked what time the fast train left, though he
must have known perfectly well. Then followed
his only risky movement. He had to drive past
the railway station, and up that alley. But the
streets were dimly lit in that part. And really
who is to tell whether a girl on the back of a
motor-bike is alive or dead, when she is fixed
firmly in place? He shot by the Dragon and
down the almost pitch dark alley-way in a
moment. It needed only seconds to lift her off
his carrier, take her to the platform, and drop
her in the river. The corpse would sink for a
time, at any rate. And when it was found—
what evidence would there be against him?
He had been seen with her just before six. He
was in the pub just after—alone. And for the
rest of the evening he meant to have an alibi.
He would be clear. But—well, the unexpected
happened, and his conscience hit harder than
he had foreseen, and he blurted out what he
had done to his adopted uncle. The rest we
know."

"It's flawless!" I exclaimed, "you've got it.
Every fact fits perfectly into place—even what
we know of Fairfax."

Stute lit a cigarette.

"I expect by now they'll have recovered the corpse," he said. "Thank heaven we're just coming in, and this case is over."

When Beef was collected and the three of us had gone down the gangway, I felt delighted. But all of us, I think, were surprised to see Galsworthy, rather too smartly dressed for a policeman, awaiting us in the Customs sheds.

"Constable!" snapped Stute, "what are you doing here?"

With his accustomed calm, Galsworthy faced the detective.

"It was my free day, sir," he said, "So I thought I would come down on my motor-bike, and tell you the news. I thought it might save you an unnecessary journey to Braxham, sir."

"Well?"

"They've found Smythe," said Galsworthy.

For the first time I saw a smile of satisfaction on Stute's face, and he turned to me as much as to say, 'I told you so.' Then he looked back to Galsworthy.

"Dead, of course," he presumed.

"Oh no, sir. Alive, in London. I can give you her address."

Stute brushed past him with a sound like a growl, and Galsworthy was left there alone while we made for the garage in which the detective had left his car.

He allowed himself one word, and it was scarcely kind to Miss Smythe.

"Damn!" was what he said angrily, as he stamped on the self-starter.

G

CHAPTER XXIII

BACK in Braxham we found that the enthusiastic Galsworthy had been rather too definite in his report. The message from Scotland Yard had been to the effect that a girl called Estelle Smythe, who answered in all respects to the description given, had been found living in Delisle Street, Leicester Square, but that she had not been questioned, pending Stute's instructions.

"Probably an entirely different woman," said Stute hopefully. "I don't know what that young fool Tennyson, or whatever his name is, wanted to come tearing down to the boat for."

"What will you do?"

"Have to run up, of course. Trouble is how we're going to identify her. I suppose there's only one way."

Beef groaned.

"Not . . . not that Walker woman?" he said.

"No help for it," said Stute. "We'll have to go and get her this afternoon."

"You won't 'ardly need me then, will you?" pleaded Beef.

"No, Sergeant," said Stute, and proceeded to telephone instructions for checking Fairfax's alibi.

That afternoon I accompanied him to Chopley to call for Mrs. Walker. This time he was undisguisedly glad to have me with him, if only as some protection from the torrents of her words. Once again as we entered the village, young Constable Smith was awaiting us. He saluted and in his rather priggishly efficient manner told Stute that he had seen Mrs. Walker, as instructed, and that she was getting ready to accompany us.

Irritated by Stute's satisfaction with Smith's efforts, as contrasted with his snubbing attitude towards Galsworthy, I spoke to the constable myself.

"You look an athletic sort of chap," I said. "You've entered for the Boxing Championship, I suppose?"

"Oh yes," he replied, "I'm in the finals. I have to meet your Braxham man, I believe."

"Galsworthy?" I asked.

"If that can really be his name," returned Smith, with something like a sneer.

I noticed that Stute was smiling to himself as we drove on to Rose Cottage.

Mrs. Walker was ready for us. Clad in an untidy coat and skirt, with a shapeless mauve felt hat on her head, she hurried down the garden path fingering a moulting squirrel boa.

"Did you send that policeman round to my house?" was her greeting to Stute as she took her place in the car. "I wish you'd be more considerate. People will begin to think that the murder took place in my front-sitting-room instead of out on the Common, as I've a hundred times told you. And why you should want me to come trapesing up to London to see some girl who can't possibly be that poor young woman who was murdered weeks ago, I can't think. But I suppose the police have got to do something to pretend to earn a living."

She was obviously enjoying the whole thing, including the car-drive, and the licence to grumble and talk to her heart's content.

"It seems extraordinary to me that you shouldn't be able to find an ordinary corpse," she went on. "It isn't as though it was something anyone might drop out of their pockets. And here we are, weeks afterwards, and nothing done. I've told you from the first he did it, the young rotter, and it's a wonder he didn't turn on me as well."

Stute sighed. "It is," he murmured rudely.

But Mrs. Walker fortunately missed the application of his remark, for adjusting a tremulous hat-pin she continued unmoved.

"It's my belief," she said, "though I didn't intend to say anything about it, that there was more than what we think between her and young Rogers. I shouldn't be surprised if she hadn't had a baby some time or another, or else she had seen him since those days and was expecting. You can't tell. But she must have had something up her sleeve, coming all this way after him. And she must have known that there wasn't much chance of her getting anything out of his having promised to marry her."

"The possibility had occured to me," said Stute dryly.

"Mind you, I'm only saying what I think. She never said anything to me about it, as you can well imagine. But where there's smoke there's fire, and he was an artful fellow if ever there was one. Why I've caught him looking at *me* in a funny way before now, and thought to myself, No, you don't. *I* wasn't born yesterday, and it's a good thing I wasn't as things turned out, for I'm sure I've no fancy for having my throat cut and left out somewhere for weeks without the police finding me to give me a decent burial as that poor girl was. And according to what you said when you came over before, she wasn't the only one, but four or five more he did for, the same day. Regular Bluebeard as you might say, like that fellow they got hold of just before the War who'd drowned all those poor girls in his bath without anyone ever knowing any different till he'd done for half a dozen. What were the police doing *then*, I should like to know? And as for that Constable Smith pestering the life out of me every day with his questions, well, I scarcely know where I am."

"Has Smith been troubling you?" Stute asked.

"It seems," I put in quickly, "that Galsworthy isn't the only over-enthusiastic policeman in the neighbourhood."

That seemed to reverse Mrs. Walker's attitude. "Not exactly troubling me, I can't say," she returned, "for I suppose he was only doing his duty. And he's as decent a young chap as you could find in the Force, take him all round." A curious giggling sound came from her. "If they was all like him I shouldn't mind so much, and him training so hard for his Boxing Match which didn't ought to be allowed, spoiling their features and that, all for nothing. But what I don't like is the uniform forever popping in and out of my cottage. People talk so, and if they don't think the murder was there they'll start saying worse of me, and then where's my business gone?"

Stute seemed to think it time to draw her gently towards the matter in hand.

"You realize, don't you, Mrs. Walker, that Scotland Yard believes that the young woman we are going to see is the one who stayed in your house, and met Rogers?"

"They can think what they like, but I know different. That poor girl's been murdered and very likely chopped up and buried weeks ago. Still, I suppose you were right to come to me, since I'm the only one to tell you for certain that this one's different. Only I hope my time's taken into consideration, for I can't go careering all over the country in motor cars with people very likely thinking I've been arrested, for nothing, as you well know. I'd be only too glad to think it *was* poor Stella Smythe, alive and well again, but what's the good when I know it isn't and so do you, if you think about it for two minutes."

We were already on the outskirts of London, but even the noise of traffic did not deter Mrs. Walker from her monologue.

"I suppose it will mean now that every time you get hold of a girl you think may be this Smythe you'll be pestering me to come and tell you it isn't. I wish to goodness you'd get the whole business settled up. I mean, it seems so ridiculous when you know who's done it not to be able to make up your minds what he's done. If I had your job for a couple of days I'm sure I shouldn't be philandering about coming to see heaven knows who, when there's a corpse to be cleared up somewhere. Besides, it will probably give this girl a nasty turn to have detectives bobbing up just when she's going to have a cup of tea. Well, this looks like Delisle Street, so I suppose we're there at last, and have got to face it out. Is this the house? I can't say I much care for the whole business. You must do the talking, of course."

"I'll try," sighed Stute, as we got out of the car.

The number given him proved to be that on a narrow doorway between two shops. A piece of paper was stuck on the woodwork beside the bells on which was written, "Please Walk Up," so that we obeyed.

On the first floor the doors seemed fairly well painted, and on several of them were visiting cards in little brass slots. But as we went higher the place grew dingier, and less cared-for.

"Nice sort of a house to bring anyone to," said Mrs. Walker bitterly. "You never know who might walk out of one of those doors. It's like a film I saw, only worse."

We reached a door on which there was a soiled piece of pink writing paper with the name "Miss Estelle Smythe" scribbled over it. Stute tapped.

Mrs. Walker beside me was breathing heavily, either from excitement or the effort of climbing the stairs. But at first no sound came from within, and Stute tapped harder.

"Wait a minute, can't you?" It was a shrill feminine voice, loud and irritable.

"Is it?" I whispered to Mrs. Walker.

"Shshsh!" she returned, her ear pressed forward, and her eyes blinking.

At last the door was opened, and I caught a glimpse of a girl with tousled hair, dressed in a kimono.

"What on earth . . . " she began, then, seeing Mrs. Walker, she gave a cry of indignation and horror, and tried to shut the door.

But Stute had pushed his foot forward. The girl shouted something. "Go away!" I think it was.

Then Mrs. Walker, nodding excitedly, exclaimed, "That's her!" with more emphasis than grammatical precision, and we all surged forward into the room.

CHAPTER XXIV

THE girl was quick to recover her self-possession.

"What's this mean?" she snapped at Stute.

Mrs. Walker came forward. "My dear, I'm so thankful to see you. I never for a moment thought but what that young rotter had done you in. I knew. . . ."

"Oh it's you, is it?" said the girl furiously. "You've brought them here have you? You dirty old swine, you! I might have known when I came to stay in your filthy house you'd do something like this. And who are these fellows? A couple of dicks, I suppose. Well, what d'you want, both of you?"

Stute stared coldly at her.

"Your name Smythe?" he asked.

"Well? If it is?"

"You were in Chopley and afterwards in Braxham on the day on which Alan Rogers committed suicide?"

"Well?"

"Then why haven't you come forward with your information?"

"Perhaps I didn't choose to."

"You know what you can be charged with, don't you?"

"I could trust you to fake something up, even if I didn't."

"No need to be cheeky. I've come to ask you a few questions, and I want civil answers."

"Hurry up and ask them, then, and leave me alone. I've got to go out."

Just for a moment I thought that Mrs. Walker was going to break in, but when she tried to talk Stute silenced her instantly. He was completely at home, and master of the situation. He took a chair placed in front of the door and turned to Smythe.

I looked round the room. It was an unpleasant example of the disadvantages of selling cheap lacquer paints. The wood-work had been done in a lavish scarlet, the walls distempered by an amateur with raspberry pink. The furniture was inexpensive, but there was an abundance of cushions in vivid colours. Behind the girl was the bed from which she had risen, presumably, to open the door.

She herself was florid and pink as her background, with bright yellow hair and too many rings. She yawned as Stute faced her.

"What's your name?"

"Smythe."

"Christian name?"

"Stella."

"Why do you call yourself Estelle then?"

"Professional name."

"Indeed. What profession?"

"Stage. Chorus lady."

"How long had you known Rogers?"

"Oh, I dunno without a lot of thinking. And I'm too sleepy to think now. A few years, anyway."

"Why did you want to see him?"

Miss Smythe yawned again. "Why do you

think?" she asked. "Just for the pleasure of a chat?"

Mrs. Walker could control herself no longer. "She was . . ."

But Stute was too quick for her.

"That's quite enough from you," he thundered.

"Oh very well. If a lady can't . . ."

Stute wheeled from her to Smythe and his voice drowned her grumbling.

"You wanted money, I suppose?"

"Well, didn't I have reason? After all . . ."

"And you got it?"

There was a pause, after which Miss Smythe seemed to think that it would be best to speak the truth.

"He did give me a little present," she admitted.

"And you gave him back his letters?"

Smythe turned on Mrs. Walker. "That's you again," she said. "What business was it of yours?"

But Stute was not going to allow arguments.

"Did you?" he repeated.

"Well, yes."

"When?"

"Before we left *her* house."

"What did he do with the letters?"

"Burnt them."

"Where?"

"On that Common place. I made him stop. I was getting bumped to death on the back of that awful machine. I wasn't used to that sort of thing. If any gentleman has wanted to take me anywhere . . ."

"That'll do. So you stopped on the Common?"

"Just for a moment. There was nothing in it."

"In what?"

"Oh, go on. You know what I mean. We only stopped for two ticks."

"But long enough for him to burn the letters?"

"Yes. He put petrol over them. Well, he didn't want to go home with them in his pocket. Then he walked back to the motor-bike."

"And rode into Braxham?"

"Well, not quite. He *would* wait just outside for a time."

"Why was that?"

"Cheek, it was. He said he wanted to slip me up to the train at the last moment. He was carrying on, as I very well knew, with that dreary little Cutler piece, and I suppose he was afraid that she or her mother would hear of it."

"Anyone come by while you were waiting?"

"No. I don't think so. Oh yes there was, though. A porter on a bicycle. Haven't you asked enough questions yet?"

"Not nearly. What happened next?"

"Nothing. He took me up to the station, and I caught the train."

"And you come right up to London?"

"Of course I did. And glad I was to get back. I never could stand the country. All slush and muck everywhere. Can't keep your shoes decent two minutes."

"Did Rogers say what he was going to do that evening?"

"He was meeting his girl, I believe."

"He didn't say anything else?"

"Not that I can remember. Why? D'you think he told me who he was going to do in?"

"Did he say anything about his having been followed?"

"Followed. No. Not to me he didn't."

"How much did he give you for the letters?"

"That's my business."

"How much?" Stute's tone never changed.

"Really. I should like to know what business you've got coming here and questioning me like this."

"How much?"

"Not much, really."

"I'm waiting."

"About £20."

"*About* £20?"

"Well, £20."

"Where d'you suppose he got that from?"

"How should I know? Though he did say something about having sold some lottery tickets or something."

"Did he say to whom he had sold them?"

"No."

"Did he mention a men called Fairfax?"

"No. Not that I can remember."

"Had you any idea that he was running drugs into the country."

"No. Indeed I hadn't. I shouldn't have approved of that. Not drugs, I shouldn't have."

"Why did he stop and buy rope in Chopley?"

"To tie my attaché case on the carrier. It

was slipping about all over the place. I told him it was dangerous."

"When you read in the papers that Rogers had murdered someone, who did you think it would be?"

"Hadn't the remotest. I know who I wish it had been," she added with a glance at Mrs. Walker.

"You say you came up to town on the six o'clock train. What proof have you?"

"Proof? What do you mean? I did come up on that train."

"What did you do when you got up here?"

"Went to see some friends of mine."

"Name?"

"I don't see why I should drag them into this."

"When I remind you that a murder was committed in Braxham that evening I think you'll understand that you had better explain your alibi—if you've got one."

That seemed to startle the girl a little. "They were Miss Renée Adair, and Mrs. Wainwright."

"Address?"

"Sixty-six Ararat Street, Covent Garden. Top flat. I was with Renée for the rest of the evening."

"Have you been in this room long?"

"A few weeks."

"Since that day, in fact. You found it advisable to change your address, instead of coming forward with what information you could."

"I didn't want to be mixed up in it."

"No. I don't suppose you did. And if every-one acted as you have our work would be twice as hard as it is now."

"Can't help your troubles," said Miss Smythe airily.

There was a pause, during which Stute seemed to be considering his future line of attack.

"Finished now?" asked Smythe. "I've got things to do, you know."

"How did you get that £20 out of Rogers? Told him there was a baby, I suppose. All right. Don't answer."

Another long pause, during which Mrs. Walker fidgeted irritably.

"Look here, Miss Smythe," said Stute sud-denly, in a more civil tone of voice, "I believe you when you say that you knew nothing about the murder. Now you won't hear any more of me after this if you'll do your best to help me now. Just rack your brains and see if you can think of anything else that might help us. Rogers left you, and went straight off, so far as we can make out, and committed a murder. Now tell us if you can remember anything he said or did that would help us."

"I'm trying to think," the girl replied. "Honestly I am. No, I really can't remember another thing. I was as surprised as everyone else when I read how he'd done for someone, and killed himself. He seemed full of beans that night."

Stute rose. "Very well then," he said, "we'll leave it at that." And he turned to go.

I thought for a moment that there was going

to be some discordance between the two women, but both seemed to prefer an attitude of exaggerated hauteur to one of violence. Mrs. Walker made her exit royally, and Miss Smythe pretended to yawn again.

Not until we were in the car, and at her mercy, did Mrs. Walker release her pent-up feelings.

"There you are!" she said. "That's what comes of being good to anyone. And to think of that girl being alive the whole time! Deceitful, I call it. She might have told anyone and saved all that searching for her. And £20 too! If I'd have known she'd got all that, things would have been very different. But there you are. Well, now you know *she's* alive, so I suppose you've got to find out who was murdered."

"Yes," said Stute, "I have. And if you would be good enough to remain silent for a moment I might have a chance of concentrating what wits I have left on the subject."

"There. That's a nice thing to say to anyone. And after I've come all this way to help you. Still, it's what one must expect from the police I suppose. I shall be glad when we're home."

CHAPTER XXV

AT dinner that night Stute was in good spirits, but I fancied that there was irony in his amusement.

"Really," he said, "this thing is going too far. It seems we have only to start enquiries for one of the people we supposed murdered, to find them safe and sound, and quite willing to tell us all they know. I've never had such a case. Do you know that for the first time in ten years I've been thinking of getting someone else in?"

"I don't think you should do that," I said. "After all, it is narrowing down."

"Narrowing down! I should think it was. It will fade away altogether soon. But what can I do? If I go to my chief and say I don't believe that anyone was murdered, he will instantly ask why young Rogers committed suicide. And whom he had stabbed with that knife. And whose blood it was. After all, even if nobody's dead, young Rogers believed there was. Where is that person?"

I sighed. "Don't ask me," I begged, "I've been out of my depth from the beginning."

"There is this about the facts that we've collected—they are gradually establishing the time of the murder. Now that we have found the girl it can be assumed that it was done

after Rogers left the Dragon at twenty to seven.
I am going to concentrate everything on the
next hour and a half—that is before he got
back to confess to old Rogers at eight o'clock.
I've instructed that constable. . . ."

"Galsworthy, do you mean?"

Stute nodded irritably. "I've sent him to
question the commissionaire and box-office girl
at the Cinema, to see if they remember Molly
Cutler waiting there at seven o'clock. And
we'll go to-morrow to see the people living on
either side of old Rogers's shop, in the hope of
discovering whether young Rogers came in
while his uncle was out between six-thirty and
seven fifteen. But it's all hearsay. All reports
from townspeople. Nothing to go on. Give
me an honest murder with a body to it, and I'll
find your man. A couple of bloodstained carpets
and a telegram from Bournemouth, and we'll
have a hanging. But damn it—where are you
in a thing like this? It doesn't need a detective
but a fortune-teller, or a water-diviner, or a
medium."

"You know very well you're enjoying it," I
said.

"Well, it's unusual. But they're getting a bit
impatient at the Yard. They need me in this
Rochester affair."

"You've still got the foreigner," I reminded
him, "and Mr. Sawyer's brother."

"And a thousand other people who haven't
been seen lately. I dislike the idea of even
making enquiries about the publican's brother.
It will make a fool of me, because no one would

believe afterwards that I wasn't certain it was
he. And also because I don't want to be the
one who sends that poor devil back to his wife.
I'm a married man myself."

"And so?"

"So we must just go on hammering away.
Collecting facts and sorting them out. At any
rate we have established that it was *not* Fairfax
and *not* the girl, who was murdered." And
again he smiled somewhat bitterly.

Next morning several reports had come in.
Fairfax's alibi was in order. The shop at which
he had bought the two hand-bags was able to
find the purchase in their books for that Wednesday, and a record of their having been sent to
Hammersmith that night. The assistant even
claimed to recognize the photograph shewn
him. The barmaid at the Sword on the Cross
remembered the incident referred to by Fairfax
and on seeing his photograph said that he often
came in. But she could not, of course, fix the
date. However, since Fairfax had been at Braxham for some days before, and had, presumably,
gone to France the morning after, this added
weight to his story. The most concise and
satisfactory confirmation came from the Flintshire Hotel, who remembered Fairfax and had
a record of his having stayed there that night
under the name of Fortescue.

"Nice 'ow it all fits in," commented Beef.

"I think we can take it as proved," Stute
admitted more dryly.

Then Galsworthy had to tell us that both
the commissionaire and the box-office clerk at

the Cinema clearly remembered Molly Cutler
having waited about in the foyer for "at least
an hour" on the day of the suicide, and had
often commented on it since. Galsworthy was
about to go into details of how upset she had
been when Stute cut him short and dismissed
him.

"'E's a decent young fellow," Beef said.
"'Is trouble is 'e keeps too much to 'imself.
Never gets among the other fellows. 'Owever,
wot with this training. . . ."

"There are more important matters to be
discussed, Beef, than the idiosyncrasies of your
assistant. Have you done as I asked you and
questioned the various garages where Rogers
might have bought petrol?"

"Yessir. 'E 'ad some in at Timkins's near the
station at some time just before three, but
that's all."

"Very well. And now we will go round and
see the people living beside old Rogers's shop, to
see whether they remember hearing the motor-
bike that night."

The houses of the High Street were old, and
as so often happens behind the clearly divided
shop fronts, the living quarters were chaotically
arranged. The yard of one house would be set
behind the back windows of another, while
behind a lock-up shop would be the whole of
a dwelling-house which was reached by a
passage running down beside it.

We went first to old Rogers himself, who
left his workshop to show us where his adopted
nephew had kept his motor-bike. Between

Rogers's shop and the next, a dingy furniture store, was a public passage leading right through to another street, and in the wall of this was a wooden doorway into Rogers's back-yard.

"He had fixed that door with a spring catch behind it, and a Yale lock, so that when he went out on his bike he left the latch of the lock up, and when he came back he had only to kick the door and it would stay open for him. You can see the place on the paint-work where he used to kick it. Then he could ride right in, across the yard, and into that shed, where he kept it. It was a heavy machine, and he didn't like wheeling it," old Rogers explained.

"Very ingenious," said Stute. "But noisy for you if you were sitting in your room behind the shop."

"Oh, we didn't mind that," said old Rogers with a smile. "We were used to noise when he was about."

"I see. So that if, when he came in at eight o'clock that evening, he had come on his motor-bike, you would certainly have known it?"

"Oh yes. But I'm sure he didn't. Unless by any chance he wheeled it in on purpose. Even if he'd ridden it up the passage I should have noticed, because it used to resound between those two walls."

"So that I am to understand that he came in on his motor-bike between half-past six and seven while you were out, and then went out again on foot?"

"That's what it certainly looks like. His bike was in the shed next morning, anyway."

"Whose windows are those?" queried Stute, indicating two very dirty windows which looked out on to the Rogers's back yard. They faced the wall with the door in it from a house behind the shop on that side.

"Some people we have nothing to do with. Well, there are a lot of children, and they took to climbing out of that window into our garden, and when I spoke to the mother about it, she got very abusive. Very abusive indeed."

"Does she own the shop in front of her house?"

"Oh no. That's a lock-up sweet shop. These premises are let to her—very cheaply I believe, but the landlord can't get her out. Not very pleasant neighbours for us. Such very dirty children. My wife gets quite worried about them."

"I see. How does one get to them?"

"There is an entrance between my shop and the sweet-shop next door."

"Thank you, Mr. Rogers."

"If you do see those people, Scuttle the name is, please don't mention us in any way. We shouldn't like any unpleasantness."

"I'll remember."

The owner of the cheerless second-hand furniture store beyond the passage proved to be rather deaf. He was stupid or obstinate or both. No, he certainly didn't know which was the night of the suicide. He didn't know there had been a suicide. He never read the papers— they were full of lies, anyway. Yes, he had heard the noise of the motor-bike in the passage often—he wasn't as deaf as all that. He couldn't remember when he had heard it last, and certainly not at what time of day. He didn't have much to do with his neighbours, and knew nothing of their goings and comings.

The sweet-shop, on the other hand, produced a tall bespectacled gentleman who would have liked to be helpful, but who closed his shop and went home every evening at six-thirty except on Saturdays, when he kept open later. He hadn't noticed young Rogers return that evening, but he suggested a call on Mrs. Scuttle next door. She had the living quarters of his shop and her windows, as we knew, overlooked the Rogers's yard. She ought to be able to tell us if anyone could.

Stute rang at her bell. There was an instant scuffle audible, and after a fight for the privilege of opening the door two very dirty little girls faced us. There was jam on their cheeks, and their clothes were stained and rather ragged.

"Where's your mother?" asked Stute.

"In the lavortree," instantly replied the taller.

Beef gave a rather vulgar guffaw behind me, but Stute remained calm. He did not need to speak again, however, for both small girls rushed helter-skelter down the passage shouting "Mum!"

Presently Mrs. Scuttle approached, her skirts clutched by several more children. She was a lean and harassed soul in her late thirties, as dirty and untidy as her children. Her dark hair looked greasy and hastily tied together.

She eyed us with some alarm, a hand on the door as if ready to shut it if our business wasn't welcome.

"Yes?" she said.

"I have come to make a few enquiries, Mrs. Scuttle," said Stute, "I think you may be able to help us. 'I am investigating this matter of young Rogers."

Mrs. Scuttle's attention was temporarily claimed by one of the children.

"Marjree!" she shrieked. "Leave off, can't you?" Then turning to us she said, "Well, you better come in. I can't stand talking here."

We followed her down the passage to a malodorous room with a kitchen range in it, before which a number of pieces of clothing were hung to dry.

"I don't know what I can tell you, I'm sure." She turned aside to a small boy. "'Orriss! Will you put that down!" Then to us again, "What is it you want to know?"

I have no idea how many children there were in that room. Sometimes, in my wilder nightmares, I think there were a dozen. There can't have been less than six. And the whole of our interview was punctuated by her violent adjurations to them.

"Oh yes. I remember the evening right enough. Well, there was good cause to, wasn't there? (Sessull! Leave 'er alone, you naughty boy. I'll get this policeman to take you away.) Yes, I 'eard 'is motor-bike come in. I said to my 'usband next morning when we 'eard what'd 'appened that I 'eard 'im come in."

"What time would that have been?"

"Well I was just putting Freeder to bed. It must 'ave been about 'arf past six. Not much later, anyway. (Roobee! You'll go to bed in a minute!) I always knew when 'e came in at night because apart from the noise 'is light used to shine right in that window."

"And would you have heard him if he went out again?"

"It's more than likely. He used to put 'is lights on in the yard, even if 'e didn't start 'is machine up there, which 'e did, as often as not. (Mind what you're doing! Erbutt, I'm speaking to you! You'll 'ave that over!) No, I'm sure 'e didn't take 'is bike out again that night. I should 'ave noticed."

That seemed doubtful in the face of the distractions which assailed her. But I supposed that she was accustomed enough to these to have been able to give her attention to the engrossing matters of her neighbours' activities.

"And you heard nothing more that night?"

"Nothing at all. I've often thought to myself that I might well 'ave, but I didn't, so that's all there was to it. (Rouse! ROUSE!) No I can't tell you what I don't know."

"Thank you, Mrs. Scuttle."

"Oh, you're welcome. I'd like to know who it was 'e did in, too. But I shouldn't be surprised if we never do know, now."

CHAPTER XXVI

"And I'm beginning to agree with her," said Stute, as we gratefully breathed fresh air again.

"Oh, come," I said, "you've got another detail in your time-table. You know now that young Rogers came in while his uncle was having his evening stroll, and went out again, presumably on foot."

"Presumably, but not certainly. Remember that old Rogers describes him as coming in at eight o'clock, with his oilskins wet and muddy. Is one to suppose that he went out wearing those oilskins, but on foot? They'd be pretty trying to walk about in."

"But on a wet night."

"Well, we shall see. At least we know that he did come in between 6.30 and 7.0 and that he brought his motor-bike into the yard behind the shop."

Stute left us soon after that, in none too good a temper. He seemed irritated, not so much because he had failed to solve the case, but because he had been baffled by a matter which had seemed so obvious. He could never forget that to the Yard it had at first not seemed worth investigation, that Beef had actually been told to clear it up himself. And he still could not reconcile himself to the fact that after these weeks of investigation he was still eluded not by a murderer but by a murder.

Beef suggested a game of darts that evening, and when we reached the Dragon we were met with still more discouraging news.

"George has turned up again," wheezed Sawyer across the counter to us.

"Who's George?" I asked Beef.

"'Is brother, wot 'ad cleared out to escape 'is wife," Beef explained.

"Yes, poor chap," said Mr. Sawyer, "I went over there yesterday and found him back in harness. It seemed she put his photo in the paper and the people where he was working saw it and it was all up with him."

Secretly I had had a fancy for Mr. Sawyer's brother as the person murdered by Rogers, so that it wasn't hard for me to disguise my disappointment by an exaggerated sympathy with the returned prodigal.

"What a shame!" I said.

"You're right. It is a shame," said the publican. "She's giving him no end of a time now she has got him back. When I was over there yesterday he didn't dare stick his head out of the door without her being after him with that tongue of hers. You ought to hear her. And one of his men's left who'd been with him for twelve years, because he said he couldn't stand the way *she's* been on to him while George was away."

"It's not right," said Beef.

"It's *not* right," agreed the publican, with even more emphasis. "She's not much better with me. Got on to me as soon as I got there yesterday for helping George when he went off.

Of course she'd got it out of him where he'd got the money from. You should have heard how she went for me over it. Ought to be in prison, she said, for helping a man to desert his wife. I was as bad as George, she said. Then she started on about keeping a public house and all that."

"And wot did you say?" asked Beef.

"Me? Well, for George's sake I didn't say much. It would only have made her worse with him after I'd gone. It turns out he's been in London, and got work almost at once on a building job in Highgate somewhere. Only the silly chap went and give his own name when they asked him, and there you are. He says he was as comfortable as anything where he was, nice rooms and that, and if he wanted to go out for half an hour in the evening there was no one to say he shouldn't."

"What time did he leave here?" asked Beef thoughtfully.

"*Here?*"

"Yes. On the night he pushed off, I mean?"

"Well, I told you. 'E came in to borrow . . ."

"Yes, I know. But wot time did 'e leave the town, I mean?"

"Oh, I can't tell you that."

"I should like to know, though."

"Why? You're not trying to mix *him* up in this murder business, are you? Because if so I can tell you right away you're talking silly. George wouldn't hurt a fly, and if he was going to do anyone in we all know who it would be."

Beef became pompous. "I 'ave to make my enquiries," he said, "without respect for persons or private feelings. I shall probably 'ave an interview with your brother before long."

"Well, go ahead and have it. And I hope she's there, that's all. I'd like to see her face when a policeman comes to the door, straight I would. I wouldn't mind coming over to Claydown to see it for myself."

"It'll be with 'im I shall want to talk," returned Beef solemnly.

Mr. Sawyer waddled off to serve someone on the other side of the bar, and I turned to Beef.

"Have you really any suspicions in this case?" I asked.

"I'm beginning to 'ave a h'inkling," he returned. "One thing I'll tell you, I don't know no more than you do. I 'aven't seen nothink nor 'eard nothink, wot you don't know of. All I've got is an idea of wot may 'ave 'appened. And if you'd thought it out same as I 'ave you'd see just as much. Only . . ." he pulled at his ginger moustache and I really began to think he was getting conceited, "only, it takes training to solve anythink like this. Training, see? Not being in the police you couldn't 'ardly be expected to've done it."

"Why hasn't Stute, then?" I asked quickly. "He's had training enough, surely?"

Beef shook his head.

"It's all these modern methods wot confuses those chaps," he said sadly, "Vucetich System, and Psy . . .sy . . ."

"Psychology?"

"That's it—Sickology. And tracing this, that, and the other. And analysis and wot not. I go on wot I been taught."

"What's that?"

"Well, if you listen to wot I'm going to tell you, you'll be able to solve these cases same as I do. Specially this case, which never needed no more than wot I know. First of all, when you find something connected with it wot you can't account for, you puzzle it out, and puzzle it out, till you do, see? That's the first thing. And the next thing is to believe nothink of wot you 'ears and only 'arf of wot you sees."

"Do you mean that our witnesses have been lying?"

"Not necessary. I mean things aren't always wot they appear to be."

"Well. Go on."

"That's about all I can explain. The rest's just experience. Police experience. You need that. Just like in this case. I don't say I know the answer. I've got a lot to make sure of before I can say that. But I've got a pretty good idea. Whereas you're all at sea. Why? No police training, that's all. You've seen and 'eard everythink just as I 'ave. And don't forget that if you make a book about it like you did about that other turn-out, don't you go and make it appear as though I kept somethink up my sleeve. I know no more than wot you do. Only I know 'ow to put it together and make somethink of it."

"Well, Sergeant. I shall be the first to congratulate you if you've got anywhere near the truth. But I can't help feeling that Sawyer's brother was your last chance."

"Sawyer's brother?" Beef laughed. "Why you didn't think it was *'im* young Rogers did for? Well, I'm blowed. You don't 'arf swallow somethink. Why I could have told you that it wasn't 'im weeks ago."

"Then it must have been the foreigner."

"Wot foreigner? Oh yes. I know 'oo you mean. Well, I shouldn't bet on that if I was you."

"Then I suppose you're going to say that there wasn't a murder at all?"

"Oh, no," said Beef quite seriously. "I wasn't going to say that. There was a murder, all right, and don't you forget it."

CHAPTER XXVII

But the last word for Stute came next morning in the shape of an air mail budget from Buenos Aires with a whole row of impressive looking Argentine stamps on it, together with an English translation which had been made in London for Stute's convenience.

"I wonder what your 'esteemed colleague' has to say this time," I said, when Galsworthy brought the thing in.

Stute rarely indulged in unnecessary conversation, and was soon studying the English document with a faint frown on his forehead. When he had finished he handed it across to me.

"Esteemed Friend," it ran,

"I thank you for your amiable communication. I was delighted to note from it that you are good enough to express some praise for our system of finger-print identification, and to hear that the information which we were most fortunately able to give you was of some service to you in your intricate and profound researches. It is always a cause of pleasure to us to find that our system enables us to assist where other systems, however excellent in their way, could not do so.

"Since I had the honour of writing to you there have been a number of developments in the case in our territory of which I think you should immediately be made aware. Not having the benefit of your full confidence in this matter we are unable to judge of the extent to which our information will serve you, but we are giving you the details herewith in the supposition that you may find them useful.

"We have succeeded in identifying and arresting the persons in Buenos Aires who were engaged in the transportation of cocaine to Great Britain. They are as follows: Elias Ipriz (51), Contumelio Zaccharetti Zibar (47), Izaak Moise Barduski (34), Julio Alejandro Carneval (62), John Whitehouse Rigby (44), Iacobi Lazaro Coetho (27).

"The subject Ipriz was the proprietor of a pharmacy, the subjects Zibar and Carneval acted as his dispensers and assistants, while the remaining persons were engaged in the difficult process of obtaining and supplying agents for the transport of the drugs.

"We have become aware that large sums were placed to the credit of Ipriz through the Paris branch of an international bank, but we are unable of course to give you any information as to the identity of the person or persons who sent these sums in this way.

"You will not think, I fervently hope, esteemed friend, that we have been dilatory or negligent in our attempts to obtain this latter information. We realized very soon that if we were able to notify you of the identity of the purchaser of these drugs the

H

information would be of the greatest use to you not only in your pursuit of the criminals who are engaged in drug-smuggling, but possibly also in your investigation of the matter of the subject Alan Rogers, about whose confession of murder we have been able to read.

"But it has been to no avail. We have questioned each of the prisoners, and used the most rigorous methods possible for the eliciting of information. But each has ardently professed that he was unaware of the identity of the person to whom they were sent. An agent of this person arrived in the city as many as twelve years ago and arranged the matter which has continued uninterrupted since then. The messengers were stewards on various boats, two of whom, if not all of whom, it appears, were ignorant of the contents of the packets they carried, and knew only that on handing them over in England they would receive a certain sum. We believe that there were at least two other stewards engaged in this work, but unless it is by chance we are not likely ever to identify them. Rogers was the only one of the men known to our prisoners by name.

"Everything therefore points to the existence in your territory of a powerful person or persons who have been for years engaged in this traffic, and it is indeed fortunate that through the foresight and swift action of one of our investigating officers we were able to discover that the subject Alan Rogers was employed by this person or persons to collect the drugs from here. It is our ardent hope, and indeed our conviction, that through the brilliant work of your department the criminals in England may now be unmasked, and the whole criminal traffic be brought summarily to a close.

"But besides the need to convey to you the above information, I have another reason for giving myself the pleasure of addressing you now. It is to report the return to Buenos Aires from England of my colleague the Subcomisario Heriberto Anselmi Dominguez who had been engaged in this case. The Subcomisario Dominguez was deputed by me, with ratification from the Sub-Jefe de Policia, to proceed to Europe as a passenger on the ship on which the subject Alan Rogers was employed as a steward.

"It was my wish that Rogers should be observed during his leave in England in the hope that it would be possible to discover to whom he handed the drugs he carried. You may wonder, my dear friend, why we did not immediately notify you of our suspicions in this matter, and of the steps which we were taking to confirm them. Our reason was simply that it is our policy in these matters to complete our case as far as possible by our own efforts before making an arrest."

At this point I could not repress a smile. And Stute, seeing to what point I had reached, joined me.

"Yes," he said, "they wanted the credit all right. They were going to come out with a sensational arrest of young Rogers when he returned to Buenos Aires, and have a complete case for us, including the receivers our end. I can almost sympathize with them. It's bad luck that Rogers should have committed suicide at that point."

"Very," I said.

"But there's worse luck than that. Read on."

"The Subcomisario Dominguez was unable to follow Rogers from the boat, as there was some confusion at the time of disembarkation. But being determined to carry out his difficult task with all his recognized ability, he discovered from the officers of the steamship company by which Rogers was employed his address in the town of Braxham, and proceeded there by train on the morning of Tuesday, February 21st. Unwilling to make any enquiry at the home of Rogers, he had no remedy but to hold himself in the principal street of the town in the hope that he might observe the man he sought. But knowing that Rogers had the habits of an alcoholic addict, he remained principally in the neighbourhood of the largest hotel.

"During the late afternoon his patience and vigilance were rewarded for he observed Rogers in the company of a young lady whom he described with enthusiasm as possessing all the charm and beauty of the famously

lovely English blonde. For the rest of that
day he was able to follow the movements
of the man Rogers who returned to his own
address alone at 11.30 p.m. The Subcomisario waited until midnight, and then,
convinced that Rogers would not again emerge,
sought a lodging. But at this point he suffered
a great disillusion for he discovered that by
an Act of Parliament the various hotels close
their doors at 10 o'clock, and that now at
midnight the entire town was within doors
and seemingly asleep. The Subcomisario describes his emotions on this discovery with
some vividness and a warmth which reflects
rather strongly on the measures of your
doubtless sagacious politicians. He appears
to have spent the night in the shelter of a
band-stand in a public park, suffering con-
siderably from the ferocity of the weather.

"On the next day, the Wednesday, however, the Subcomisario with relentless deter-
mination returned to his duties, and saw the
man Rogers emerge from the shop at which
he lived. The time was approximately 10.30.
The man was on a motor-bicycle. Again at
2.20 the Subcomisario, at his observation
point near the most important drinking-house
of the town, saw Rogers enter with a middle-
aged man, and followed them into the bar.
Such was their air of guilt, and so rapid was
their exit when they saw him, that the Subcomisario is convinced that the elder man was
involved in the traffic in noxious drugs. He
followed the two of them, saw the older man

go towards the railway station, and Rogers take his motor-bicycle from the grounds of a private hotel nearby.

"He did not again see the subject Alan Rogers until some time after eight o'clock that evening when he saw him making once again for the Mitre Hotel. The Subcomisario remained outside for some minutes, and saw the blonde girl, whom he describes with a lyric ardour, approaching the hotel alone. He is surprised at this as his experiences have hitherto been limited to his own country where it would be highly unusual for a young lady to enter a bar, least of all unaccompanied. However, she had scarcely entered when a number of people began to emerge chattering excitedly. The Subcomisario had not a great enough command of your delightful if complex language to gather what was the cause of their emotion, however.

"Soon the young lady herself emerged, assisted by an older and heavier woman, and evidently suffering from some considerable strain. The Subcomisario raised his hat and asked courteously the cause of the excitement, but was met by an angry retort. He had therefore no alternative but to remain in the vicinity of the hotel until the man he was watching should appear. In spite of the arrival and departure of a number of persons, all seeming under some stress, he saw no sign of Rogers until very late in the night, when to his astonishment he saw the man borne out by the publican and another elderly person of rather unintelligent aspect whom he reluctantly identified as the local Sergeant of Police. A further person was with them, but the Subcomisario was unable to decide on his identity or connection with the matter.

"He was able, however, to follow this cortège into the yard at the back of the hotel, and to see Rogers placed on a settee in a bare room. He concealed himself in the urinal while the bearers entered the house. He was under the impression that Rogers was inebriated but considered it his duty to confirm this belief. He waited therefore until the household was asleep, then entered by the window of the room in which Rogers lay, finding the catch of the window of a type which he describes as constructed for the benefit of intending burglars. He had just made the discovery that the subject Alan Rogers was dead when he was disturbed by the approach of someone from the room above, whose clumsy attempt to cross the floor unheard had been only too clear to him. He left the premises, slept for an hour or two in the bandstand afore-mentioned, and returned to London by an early train. He was then confined to his room with a severe attack of influenza due to exposure and under-nourishment. He congratulated himself that he did not contract pneumonia.

"All these details, dear friend, I give you in the hope that they may assist your investigation, though I feel that by the time you receive this your researches will have terminated successfully.

"Allow me to salute you,

"Your friend and colleague,

"JULIO MORENO MENDEZ."

"Well," I remarked, not very intelligently perhaps, "that about settles it. Everything complete except a murder. It all fits in like a jigsaw. Fairfax, Smythe, Sawyer, the foreigner, all accounted for. What now?"

Stute slammed on his hat rather viciously. "Only one thing for it," he said. "I must go to the Yard and report."

PART THREE

CHAPTER XXVIII

WITH Detective-Inspector Stute out of his territory, for the moment, anyway, Beef became suddenly conspiratorial.

"Now's the time," he croaked to me, unconsciously assuming the manner of the villain in a melodrama.

"The time for what?" I asked sceptically.

"Why—for seeing if I'm right," he said. "I told you I was on to somethink."

I sighed. "Well, why don't you go ahead, if you think you can succeed where Stute failed."

"I don't say that," said Sergeant Beef, "I don't say that at all. 'E was 'ot stuff, Stute was. I daresay in a really complicated case 'is methods would be wonderful. But this 'ere's not so complicated, if wot I think turns out right. It's as simple as A B C. The big mistake I made was ever to've thought it was tricky, and 'ad 'im down here at all. I could 'ave settled it on me own weeks ago. Still, there you are. I must get to work."

"What are you going to do?"

"I'm going over to Claydown."

"To Claydown? That's where Sawyer's brother lives, isn't it?"

"That's right."

"But surely . . ."

"Now look 'ere, Mr. Townsend. Up to now there 'asn't been nothink I've knowed wot

I 'aven't told you. And I've got it all worked out. All I'm going for now is confirmation, see?"

"Oh, very well. Do you want me to come?"

"I don't 'ardly see 'ow you can, seeing as I'm going on the back of Galsworthy's motor-bike."

"Oh."

"Still," continued Beef, as though he hated to disappoint me, "if it all turns out like I think it will, you shall be in on it. Are you going to be in the Mitre this afternoon?"

"I rather thought of returning to town," I said.

"Now don't do that, Mr. Townsend. Don't go and do that just when I'm going to move decisive. You 'ang on in the hotel, and I'll ring you up soon as ever I know where I am. 'Ow's that?"

Rather unwillingly I agreed, and saw Beef seated awkwardly on the pillion of his constable's motor-cycle. I watched Galsworthy kick the starter, and they banged off down the High Street.

On my way back to the hotel it occurred to me that I should like to call in and see the old Rogers couple. Now that they had had some weeks in which to get over the first strain there was not the embarrassment one had felt at first. And I liked them, and found the warmth of their regard for the wastrel who was dead a moving thing.

The old man came forward from his work-room.

"Good morning. I've really come more or less to say good-bye," I told him.

"Are you going back to town then? I'll call my wife." And he disappeared for a moment, and returned with Mrs. Rogers.

"So you're leaving us?" she said with a smile, almost as radiant as the one I had seen on her face on that first day when she had leaned out of the carriage window to greet her husband.

"Yes," I said. "Detective-Inspector Stute went back to London yesterday. He seems quite baffled."

Mrs. Rogers looked serious. "So I suppose we shall never know what Alan did? And he'll be branded as a murderer without it ever being found out whether he struck in self-defence, or what it was. It seems a wicked thing."

"Oh, I don't think Stute has given up," I said. "He's not the man to do that. And Sergeant Beef is still on the case."

"Yes . . . but . . . of course, he's a good policeman and all that. But I don't see how it's to be expected that he'll get to the bottom of this when the London detective has failed."

I smiled, and a little tardy loyalty to my old friend prompted me to say, "I don't know. He's not a fool. He has a way of plodding on and coming out with something quite unexpected. As a matter of fact he thinks he understands this case now. He's gone over to Claydown to-day for what he calls confirmation of his theory."

"Oh well. We can only hope for the best. I should like our boy's name to be cleared as much as possible."

"I don't think you should set your hopes on that, Mrs. Rogers. The Sergeant admits that there doesn't seem to be much doubt of that part of the case. And now I must say good-bye. I'm off to-morrow."

They shook hands with me, and, feeling warmed by my visit, I returned to the Mitre for lunch.

Frankly I did not expect much of a phone call from Beef. I comforted myself with the reflection that whether it came through or not I should be acting according to the best precedents. Even if he rang through to say that he had unearthed the weeks-old corpse of young Rogers's victim, I should only be in the convention if I had long given up hope of his solving the riddle.

At about three-thirty, however, I was called to the phone.

"'Ere, Mr. Townsend," came his voice, so loud that it hurt my ear-drum and I had to hold the instrument an inch from my head, "I'm on to it all right. Got everythink mapped out. Just wot I thought."

"Well, who did he murder?" I asked, rather irritably.

"You wait till I tell you the 'ole story. It'll raise the 'air off your 'ead. I'll be with you as soon as I can. We're just starting off now. I'll pick you up at the Mitre."

"Why? Where are we going?"

"You'll see. There's one or two jobs to be done in Braxham. Then we'll pop up to the Yard, see?"

And before I could enquire any further, he had put down his receiver. He had evidently been in a state of tremendous excitement for I had heard his breath wheezing as though he were exhausted from running to the telephone. I decided to keep an open mind on the subject, and sat down to an early cup of tea to pass the time until he arrived.

When the motor-bike pulled up outside, I found myself quite unthrilled. I can see now that this was the surest proof that I had never really believed in Beef. Here he was, arriving at the Mitre with what he claimed was a proven explanation of the whole thing, and I didn't even feel inclined to go out and meet him.

He burst into the room where I still sat over the tea-things. He had, it seemed, been a bit shaken and chilled by his ride on Galsworthy's pillion, for his nose and gills were positively purple, and the fringes of his moustache were damp.

"Come on!" he almost shouted.

But I was calm. "Have a cup of tea?" I suggested.

"No time for tea. I tell you I'm right on to it. I've only got to get a bit more evidence. . . . Are you coming?"

I rose slowly. "I suppose so," I said, and followed him out.

He dismissed Galsworthy with a hurried gesture, and strode off down the High Street.

"Where are we going?" I asked wearily.

"To Rogers's shop."

"Look here, Sergeant, if you're going to start all that going round questioning people again, you can count me out. I've had enough of it with Stute."

"You can please yourself," said Beef as he hurried on.

Somehow I found myself following. I didn't believe he had solved the riddle, I was thoroughly fed up with the whole thing. But I kept with him.

As soon as I entered the bootmaker's shop for the second time that day, I knew that at least something unusual was happening, for Mrs. Rogers, looking worried, came forward excitedly.

"Oh, Sergeant," she said, "I'm so glad you've come. I was wondering whether I ought to send for you. It's my husband."

"Wot about 'im?"

"He's gone. I've never known him to act so strangely before. It must have been half an hour ago. He suddenly came downstairs dressed in his best suit, with his bag packed. I'd heard him moving about overhead, but I'd never thought anything of it. I asked him whatever he was about and he said he had to go away for a few days. I couldn't make it out. Of course he's been acting a bit strange ever since we knew about Alan. Well, it was a big blow to both of us. But to pack up and leave . . ."

"Ever know 'im to clear off like this before?"

"No. Never. Not since we've been married.
I can't understand it. Of course I've sometimes
had a fancy that Alan may have told him that
evening who it was he murdered. And perhaps
my husband can't bear the thought of it. It
may have played on his nerves like. I don't
know. It's frightened me. Suppose he loses
his memory or something? What ought I to
do?"

"But didn't 'e tell you where 'e was off to?"

"Not a word. I must have asked him a
dozen times. He wouldn't say a word. That's
what makes it so strange. And there's another
thing . . . only I don't know whether I ought
to tell you this. . . ."

"Come on, Mrs. Rogers . . ." was all
Beef needed to say.

"Well, it's this. There's a drawer in his
writing-desk that he always kept locked. I
used to pull his leg about it. And he'd laugh,
but he'd never say what was in it. Then one
day, some time before Alan came home, he
was alone at his desk when the postman called,
and he went out to get the letters, and left
the drawer open. He had some business letters
he was reading and somehow or other forgot
to lock the drawer. And when he went out
that evening I couldn't help having a peep.
And what do you think? There was a bundle
of notes there that thick—pound notes they
were—and a bit of paper under the elastic
band with £100 written on it. I *was* surprised.
Then I guessed what it was—he'd been saving
up for something for me that I wasn't to know

about. I remember he once talked of our having a baby motor car one day, and perhaps that was it. Anyway, I knew it would disappoint him if he thought I'd seen, so I said nothing about it."

"Well?" asked Beef.

"Oh yes. I was going to tell you. Just before you came I went to the drawer. I don't know what made me. But anyway I did, and the bundle was gone. I don't know what to make of it, though I daresay you do. Perhaps someone's stolen them and he's gone after him. Perhaps . . . perhaps it's something to do with Alan. Anyway, they've gone."

"All £1 notes you say?" asked Beef.

"Yes."

"New ones?"

"No. Not extra. Just ordinary, as though they'd been put there from time to time."

"Well now, Mrs. Rogers, don't you worry your 'ead off," said Beef. "I daresay every-think'll turn out for the best. Wot's the time? Quarter to six? We shall 'ave to 'urry. I wonder if you'd do me a favour now?"

"Certainly I will. What is it?"

"You 'op round to my 'ouse and tell my missus I more than likely shan't be back to-night. And if you don't like staying on your own, you get 'er to make you up a bed there, see? Now then, Mr. Townsend, we must go."

CHAPTER XXIX

AT this point I began to be infected with some of Beef's excitement. It did seem so very odd that little Mr. Rogers should have suddenly deserted his wife and his business just when the Sergeant wanted to question him again. It would have been odd at any time, but just this evening, with Beef making straight for his shop, it was uncanny.

And the Sergeant's own movements now became eccentric, to say the least of it. He almost ran down the few yards of the High Street that separated us from the chief garage of the town, and dived into its office. In a few moments the proprietor's son had driven out the old Morris Oxford that he used for taxi work, and we climbed into it.

"Drive down to the station," said Beef, "and right up close to the goods entrance. Quick as you can."

The old car moved off, and Beef sat puffing impatiently and staring out of the window, till we approached the station yard.

"Now then, Mr. Townsend," he said, "duck down. Right out of sight, please."

I obeyed, not without feeling somewhat ridiculous to find myself crouching down in the taxi with Beef on all fours beside me.

"'Arry!" he called to our driver, when the car was at a standstill. "Anyone about?"

"Not at the minute," said Harry.

"No one looking out of the waiting-room?"

"No. And they couldn't see here if they was."

"All right. We'll make a dash for it."

And suddenly, with quite unbelievable agility, old Beef had leapt from the taxi, and into the luggage office. As swiftly as possible I followed him.

Once inside he turned to the clerk there.

"Sorry," he said, "only it's important, see."

The clerk grinned. "Whatever are you up to, Sarge?" he asked, "jumping in 'ere like that?"

"No larfing matter," said Beef, and seeing Charlie Meadows, the porter who had already given evidence, he called across to him. Meadows approached.

"'Ere, Charlie," Beef said, in an exaggerated undertone, "I'm on to somethink."

His whole demeanour was that of a music-hall comedian doing a comic detective act.

"Oh yes," said Charlie Meadows laconically. He couldn't forget how his evidence had been treated before.

"I want you to do somethink for me. 'Ave a look on the platform and see if old Rogers is going on this train."

"I don't need to look. I know he is. I saw him just now."

"You did, did you? What did I tell you? Now look 'ere, Charlie. You go, and when the train comes in speak to 'im civil and put 'im in the front part of the train, see?"

"Why?"

"Never mind why. It's a matter of life and death. Will you do it?"

"I don't mind," admitted Charlie.

"Well, the train'll be in in a minute. You better go out there ready. 'Ere, Jack!" This was to the clerk. "Slip through and get us a couple of tickets to London, will you? I don't want me and Mr. Townsend to be seen."

Jack good-naturedly agreed, not without telling Beef that he was becoming a regular Sherlock Holmes. Personally I felt thoroughly ashamed of Beef. All this exaggerated secrecy, these loudly whispered instructions and surreptitious behaviour, struck me as ridiculous. I did not blame the clerk for being amused at him. However, I had thrown in my lot with the investigation, however crude its methods, and I felt I had to remain.

When the train was audible (it was the 6.0 fast train for London) Beef sent the clerk to the door which led out on to the platform.

"'As 'e got 'im?" he asked anxiously, hovering about behind the clerk, as the train came in.

"Yes. He's leading him off now."

"This is our chance then," said Beef, and as though he were a soldier advancing under fire he rushed across the platform into a third-class carriage. I could do nothing but follow.

An uncomfortable moment ensued. The carriage Beef had entered, the one nearest to the luggage-office, happened to be one of the few on the train which was more or less crowded, and the people in it showed their displeasure at having to make room for Beef when they thought it would have been easy for him to choose an emptier carriage. But he seemed oblivious of the irritated noises with which they squeezed together. He was flushed now, and his eyes had none of the glassy and sleepy look they so often showed in the morning.

Seeing the clerk lounging in the doorway, Beef stood up and let the window down, indifferent to the mumbled protests of the other passengers. Without putting his head out he beckoned Jack across.

"All right. All right," he said, when the young clerk approached, "don't look as though you was watching and telling anyone what you can see. Did the old boy turn round as we 'opped across?"

"No. He was following Charlie."

"Any sign of 'im now?"

"Yes. He's got his head stuck out of a carriage window, watching the entrance to the platform."

"I thought so," chuckled Beef. "Smart bit of work that was. 'E'll never know 'e's being followed now. Thank you, Jack. See you soon, I 'ope."

And not until the train was actually in motion did he consent to close the window and sit down.

That was one of the most uncomfortable journeys I have ever made. It is never pleasant to be surrounded by hostility, least of all when you feel that it is merited. And the self-satisfied smile which seemed to be fixed on Beef's face made things no easier.

Besides, I was puzzled. What reason could old Rogers have for this departure? It seemed likely that the old boy knew something, and perhaps had known it all along, which was to his adopted nephew's discredit. He had been determined, I supposed, not to reveal it, and something in Beef's actions to-day—his visit to Claydown, probably—had told Rogers that enough was coming to light to make it hard for him to deny his knowledge—whatever it was.

Or else, and this seemed more sinister, perhaps, whatever forces lay behind all this, the real head of the drug-smuggling gang (if such a person existed), or someone else powerful and dangerous, had some reason for not wishing old Rogers to be questioned, and had frightened him out of Braxham.

Or—yet another possibility—it might be that old Rogers knew from Beef's visit to Claydown that he was no longer the only one to know his secret. In that case he was determined to reveal it voluntarily to Scotland Yard itself, and Beef's hurry was to prevent his doing so.

In any of these cases, why had Beef insisted on the old man's being put in the front of the train? Did some danger threaten the boot-maker? And what had the £100 in £1 notes to do with it?

I would have given a very great deal to have put some of these questions to Beef but it was clearly impossible now. He would either have answered conspiratorially, in his absurdly audible stage whisper, or would pompously have reminded me that these were official secrets, and not to be discussed in public. Altogether I was greatly relieved when the train steamed in to the London station.

Beef's next action really shocked me, and I was impelled to apologize for it. The train had scarcely stopped when he pushed in front of the other passengers, including two ladies, and started off down the platform. I murmured what I could to excuse him, and secretly hoped I should never set eyes on any of those people again.

"There 'e goes," said Beef exultantly, when I reached his side.

I began to remonstrate with him for his manner of leaving the carriage but he didn't seem to hear me.

"Keep well back," he said. "Don't let 'im get 'is peepers on you, but don't lose sight of 'im neither."

Old Rogers, looking unfamiliar in a "Sunday Best" suit and bowler hat, was ahead of us, making for the barrier. I did as Beef told me, and watched his progress, without taking any risk of being observed. Right out into the hall of the station he walked, carrying his own suit-case, then seemed to hesitate for a moment and look about him. At last we saw him go into a telephone booth.

"Now's our chance!" said Beef.

I was rather tired of that phrase of his.

"Whatever for?" I asked.

"Why, to 'ave a drink, of course. We can see from the bar when he comes out of there."

"Suppose he comes to the bar?"

Beef laughed outright.

"Wot, ole Rogers?" he said. "Strick tee-totaller."

So I followed Beef to the bar, smiling at his peculiar way of walking. It was almost as though he crossed that station hall on tiptoe.

He was right though. From my position near the door I saw old Rogers emerge from his phone-box and make for the tea-room on the other side of the platform. But we could not trust to his delaying in there for it was just possible that he was working to elude us. We kept an eye on the entrance while we swallowed our drinks, and were greatly relieved when he eventually emerged.

Once again Beef started walking as though he were barefoot and the floor of the station was hot.

"You're not stalking a rabbit," I reminded him. "And I wish you'd explain what we're up to anyway."

"It won't be long before you see for your-self."

But it was five minutes before anything happened at all. The old bootmaker stood on the curb outside the station apparently watching the street, and we stood near the booking office watching him.

Suddenly Beef clutched my arm.

"There you are," he said. "Wot did I tell you?"

"What *did* you tell me?" I asked for I had seen nothing.

Then I realized what he meant. A long blue saloon car of royal proportions, of a make that can be hired with a chauffeur for the evening by those who can afford it, had drawn up by the curb, and old Rogers was speaking to the driver.

"Good Lord!" I exclaimed. It was the most surprising thing that had yet happened.

But Beef had no time to express his astonishment. No sooner had the car moved on than he had rushed for a taxi.

"Follow that blue car," he said.

"What the big——?" asked the driver naming the make.

"That's 'im. Don't go an' lose 'im now. I'll see you're all right out of it."

We had been fortunate enough to get a new taxi with a competent driver, and by the time we had reached the first set of traffic lights we were right on the other car's tail.

CHAPTER XXX

THE big car was going Southwards.

"Do you know," I said after a quarter of an hour, "I shouldn't be surprised if he's making for Croydon."

"No more shouldn't I," agreed Beef. "'E'd be off in an aeroplane if I wasn't going to stop 'im."

"But why?" I asked impatiently. "Why is he so anxious to get away?"

I could not reconcile myself to the incongruity of that mild little bootmaker dashing towards the air-port in a great hired car, dressed up in his Sunday suit, and with a battered suitcase in his hand.

"Is he so frightened of being questioned?" I went on, since there was no answer.

"I shouldn't say frightened, exactly," said Beef.

"Or is it . . . " I began more excitedly as a sudden thought struck me, "that he wants to see Fairfax? Does he know something against Fairfax? Does he want to find out something from Fairfax?"

"Now, Mr. Townsend," said Beef, "you know very well I can't go telling you everythink. You've 'ad as much chance as wot I 'ave to get at the truth until this morning. I'm not going to tell you no more. It wouldn't be etiquette."

"At least you can tell me how you're going to stop him leaving," I returned. "If he really is making for Croydon he's certain to have his passport in order. How do you think you're going to prevent his crossing?"

"Ah," said Beef, "that's where you come in."

"I?"

"Yes. You'll 'ave to charge 'im."

"Charge him? What with?"

"For pinching a 'undred pounds off of you, all in one pound notes, wot 'e 'as secreted on 'is person at this minute."

I exploded. "Don't be a fool, Beef!" I said. "D'you think I'm going to pay out thousands of pounds, when he proves that he was wrongfully arrested."

Beef gave a self-satisfied chuckle. "'E won't do that," he said, "you trust to me."

"I shouldn't consider it," I said. "To charge a man with stealing! You ought to be ashamed of yourself as a policeman suggesting such a thing."

Beef coughed. "If I could tell you everythink I'm blowed if I wouldn't, but I can't, not at this point. But I'll tell you two things, Mr. Townsend. That ole gent in the car in front knows 'oo was murdered, and 'as done all along. And life or death depends very likely on 'is not getting away from England to-night. Now, you've got to 'elp me. I wouldn't take no chances of you losing a lot of money. You won't lose nothink. On'y you've got to charge 'im, see? It's the way to 'old 'im back. You wouldn't like to feel that when a man's life or death depended on it you was found wanting would you?"

Frankly, I was bewildered. I had some idea of the seriousness of a step such as Beef wanted me to take. But on the other hand he seemed so sure of himself.

"Are you absolutely certain you're right about this?"

"Yes."

"Have you got proof?"

"Certainly I 'ave."

"And you say old Rogers has known all along?"

"That's right."

"And there is no chance whatever of my getting into trouble for doing what you ask?"

"No there isn't."

"Well, I suppose I shall have to do it."

"Thank you, Mr. Townsend. That'll be a *real* 'elp."

I didn't like the implication of his emphasis, but I let that pass. There was now little doubt that we were making for Croydon. The traffic was not so thick here, and Beef had leaned forward to tell our taxi-driver to keep some distance between ourselves and the big blue car in front, lest we should be observed. However the blind had been pulled down at the back of the saloon car so that there was little chance of this.

There is always something stirring about pursuit—even when it is no more than the pursuit of so meagre a quarry as our little boot-maker. It may be, as Stute had indicated when he arranged for the formation of a search party, some primitive hunter's instinct which takes hold of us. But I am sure that old Beef and I, sitting side by side in our taxi, felt the thrill of it when at last we reached the air-port and saw the big car turn in to it.

"Now then," said Beef, "you 'ad that 'undred quid in your room at the 'otel to-day. You saw old Rogers coming out with some excuse about looking for you. When you got in you found 'em gone. You went after 'im but 'is wife said 'e'd left for Croydon. See?"

"I see," I replied dubiously. "But it sounds pretty weak."

"It'll do for the minute," said Beef, "'specially when they find the notes on 'im."

The little man was paying the smart and gentlemanly driver of his large car.

"'Old on a minute," said Beef to our taxi-man, "We'll wait till 'e goes inside. There's police standing there."

We did. As soon as old Rogers had entered our taxi drew up, and we followed him.

The next few minutes are very vivid to me. I may have over-acted a trifle. I think perhaps now that in my excitement I did so. But I was anxious to be convincing. It is not altogether easy to make an accusation sound credible when you are charging an elderly and well-established bootmaker with having stolen £100 from you, when you know perfectly well that you had never carried this sum in notes. I dashed across the station, and, as I afterwards realized, forgot even my grammar in the urgency of the moment.

"That's him!" I shouted.

Several passengers turned towards me, and I was thankful to see that two policemen who had been chatting in the discreet manner of the police, with their eyes on the people about them, had turned to watch me.

"Stop him!" I went on, at the top of my voice.

One of the policemen now slowly came across.

"What's the matter?" he asked.

I pointed at the narrow back of old Rogers, who had remained apparently oblivious of the shouts behind him.

"That man!" I said. "He's a thief. I want to charge him!"

And now, for the first time, the bootmaker turned. He saw that I was indicating him and stopped. But he was ten yards away, and when I dropped my voice to address the policeman, he could not hear me.

"He stole a hundred pounds from me this afternoon, in one pound notes. I heard he was coming to Croydon and I've followed him here."

"Ah!" said the policeman non-commitally.

We started walking towards old Rogers who stood looking rather pathetic and dumb-founded, with his suit-case still in his hand. When we came up to him he was the first to speak.

"Why, Mr. Townsend, whatever's the matter?" he asked, staring at me wide-eyed.

I felt rather wretched as I turned to the policeman.

"My name is Stuart Townsend," I said, "I've been staying at Braxham where this man has a shop. . . ."

The constable broke in. "Before we go any further," he said to old Rogers, "I'd like to know your name."

"Rogers," said the old chap.

"Mr. Rogers, what money have you on you?"

"I can't see what concern that can be of yours," said old Rogers. He spoke not indignantly but in a puzzled voice, as though he really would have liked to know.

"Well, there's a mix-up here," was all the explanation he got, "and it would simplify things if you'd tell me."

"I have . . . some treasury notes. I really don't know how many."

"Any objection to my seeing them?"

For a moment I thought that he was going to refuse. He glanced first at me, then at the policeman.

"You may look," he said, and plunging his hand into an inside pocket he drew out a thick bundle.

The policeman turned to me.

"Are these yours?" he asked.

"They look like it," I was wise enough to say. "I had a packet of a hundred in my bedroom at the hotel to-day. At three o'clock I went upstairs and found this man coming out of the room. I looked in the drawer where I kept them, and found them gone. I am sure enough to charge him."

"You are?"

"Absolutely."

"Very well." He turned to old Rogers. "I shall have to arrest you," he said.

The old man hadn't spoken a word since I had made my preposterous accusation. And to my surprise he said nothing now. He stared at me with an expression which I find hard to describe. It was not of surprise so much as of wonder. It was as though he were trying in his mind to settle some question about me.

The policeman turned to his colleague for a moment and I contrived to draw near to the old boy. I could not bear to let him feel as he must do about me.

"It's all right," I whispered, "Beef says it's all right. He says it's a matter of a human life."

He stared at me no longer but with a shrill and angry voice began to address the police. It seemed that my brief sentence, which had been meant to calm him, had had the opposite effect. He stormed at us. It was a trumped-up accusation, he said. I was an impostor. He was a respectable tradesman of many years standing who was going for a well-merited holiday. It was scandalous that he should be delayed in this way. The policeman and I would answer for it.

I have never had more respect and gratitude for the laconic obstinacy of the police. The constable had decided to arrest old Rogers, and arrest him he did. In fact, it seemed that if he needed any more to convince him of the validity of the charge the old man's indignation provided it.

I

"Come along," he said unsympathetically, and I saw old Rogers led briskly away.

Beef was waiting for me in a great state of pleasure and excitement.

"You wasn't 'arf good!" he said, slapping me too heavily on the back. "You ort to've been an actor! The way you ran arfter 'im! I shall never forget it." He chuckled. "And charged 'im prop'ly you did. I was larfing fit to bust myself when I saw them take 'im orf!"

This praise from Sergeant Beef would have been more pleasant if he had been a dramatic critic instead of a policeman. As it was I was conscious of having done a very dubious thing, and one which might land me into all sorts of trouble.

"Thank you," I said coldly. "And now I think you owe me some explanation."

"All right. All right. You shall 'ave all the explanation you want. And *your* part in this shan't be forgotten, Mr. Townsend."

"I should much prefer that it were," I said feelingly.

"No you wouldn't—not when you know the 'ole truth. And you shan't be kep' waiting much longer for that. We're orf to Scotland Yard now. I'm going to make my report. I just rung up Inspector Stute and 'e'll be waiting for us."

"That's good," I said, but without any enthusiasm, as we got into our waiting taxi. We were soon humming back towards town.

CHAPTER XXXI

"Well now," said Beef, when we were sitting in Inspector Stute's office at Scotland Yard, "I'd like to get this job done with. I'm not much of an 'and at telling 'ow I come to get on to anythink, but I'll do my best, and be as quick as I can." He consulted a large silver watch. "There was a chap come through Braxham the other day wot said 'e always 'ad a game of darts at night in the Bricklayers' Arms, off the Gray's Inn Road, and I should like to get round and see him before they close."

"Am I to understand Beef," put in Stute impatiently, "that you really believe you've got to the bottom of this case?"

"That's it, sir."

"You know who was murdered?"

"Yes. I know 'oo was murdered."

"Then where's the corpse?"

"Buried, sir."

"Good heavens. Are you . . . ?"

"Suppose you let me start at the beginning. We shan't never get done this way. I'll try to tell it as it came to me."

"Very well," snapped Stute, interested, in spite of himself.

"Of course, sir, with all the advantages you gentlemen up 'ere 'ave over us nowadays—and Gawd knows you 'ave got them, with all these

new methods and that—there's one way we
come out strong in a case like this. That's
knowing the people in our own districts. I
mean, you understands their sick . . . sick . . ."

"Psychology?" I whispered.

"That's it. You understands all that—but
we knows their natures. It 'elps, as you'll see.
The very first thing I thought to myself about
this case was—what was young Rogers doing
committing suicide like that."

"A very profound reflection, Beef."

"Thank you, sir. What I mean is, he wasn't
the one to think it out a long way a'ead. I
know 'im well. 'E was a crazy young bounder,
always up to somethink. But 'e wasn't one to
'ave no morbid thorts about doing 'isself in.
Very well then, 'ow 'ad 'e got 'old of that
poison?"

"It didn't occur to you, I suppose, that a
man who had for years been smuggling large
quantities of cocaine into the country would
have facilities for obtaining a few grains of
cyanide of potassium?"

"Oh yes it did," returned Beef. "''E'd 'ave
'ad the facilities all right. But wot would 'e
'ave wanted it for? 'E couldn't 'ave made no
money out of bringing it in, because it's cheap
enough over 'ere without that. And if 'e'd
never 'ad no idea of suicide, why should 'e
'ave bothered to buy it abroad?"

"Since the murder was committed with a
knife I don't *quite* see what you're driving at,"
said Stute.

"You will in a minute," returned Beef calmly.

"The next thing that made me think was that suit of overalls I told you about, wot was 'anging in young Rogers's room. 'Is Aunt said 'is uncle 'ad bought them for 'im, but they'd all 'ad a larf, because they was too small. I couldn't understand that. They was careful ole people, the Rogers, not skinflint, but careful 'ow they spent their money. 'Ow 'ad 'is uncle come to make that mistake in buying them overalls? 'E *must* 'ave known that young Rogers would want the big size. Whatever 'ad possessed 'im to do that?"

"I could give you half a dozen explanations. The assistant in the shop where he bought them could have wrapped up the wrong suit."

"Admitted," said Beef grandiosely. "Admitted. I'm not giving you evidence yet, sir. I'm just telling you wot put me on to it.

"See, I've always been told that when there's something you can't understand in a case, you've got to go on figgering it out and figgering it out, till you *do* understand. And that's wot I did with those overalls as you shall 'ear when I get to it. Then there was another thing." Beef leaned forward. "Wasn't it a bit funny that Mrs. Rogers should 'ave stayed the night with Mrs. Fairfax? I mean we know what those Fairfaxes' game was. It struck me as funny at the time."

Stute sighed, but said nothing.

"And then there was that bit about young Rogers's coming in while 'is uncle was out for 'is walk, and going out again. I didn't much like the sound of that. It was a funny sort of a night for the old man to go for a walk on, anyway. And then we know from that lady with them children that young Rogers come in on 'is bike between 'arf past six and seven. Old Rogers says 'e came in again in 'is mackintoshes about eight. Wot was 'e doing all that time with them 'eavy oilskins on? 'E wasn't in no pub or we should 'ave 'eard of it. Where was 'e and wot was 'e up to?

"Last of all there was that nice young lady. Why didn't 'e meet 'er like 'e'd promised? 'E could 'ave. 'E got to 'is 'ome before seven, and it's not five minutes from the Cinema where 'e was meeting 'er. Wot made 'im not pop round?"

Still Stute said nothing.

"Those were the things that made me think," confessed Beef. "An' I thort and thort."

"Excellent," Stute said, "and your conclusions?"

"You must excuse me, sir," said Beef. "I don't 'ardly know 'ow to present the matter. I think I'll 'ave to start at the other end of the story. Now don't get impatient. I'll get on as fast as I can."

Stute nodded.

"'Ave you ever thort, sir, where the cleverest criminals are found? They're not found in criminal meeting-places, nor yet living in luxury wot no one can understand 'ow they can afford. They're found, like Crippen and Seddon and them, living just ordinary and doing a everyday job as though nothink was going on. Well, that's the kind of criminal old Rogers was."

"Old Rogers?" I gasped.

"You 'eard," said Beef. "I ain't arf glad I got on to 'im. If ever there was a proper ole scoundrel it was 'im. 'E'd been bringing in drugs for years and years. When you come to go into it you'll find 'e's got a fortune tucked away somewhere. Even Fairfax, 'oo only worked for 'im, is rich enough to retire. But ole Rogers had the sense to keep on with 'is trade. Nice old bootmaker wot everyone thort the world of. But not me. Soon as ever I 'eard 'e was a tee-totaller I 'ad my eye on 'im. I never trust 'em. Never."

"I suppose that eventually we shall come to some evidence?" queried Stute.

"Proof, not evidence," promised Beef, and continued.

"About seven years ago this respectable ole shopkeeper wot 'ated the very thort of beer, but didn't mind selling people drugs, was working in 'is shop in Bromley when in walks a young chap down and out. When 'e tells the ole chap 'is story Rogers isn't 'arf interested. 'E's been a steward on a boat going to South America. 'E's been in jug. And 'e 'asn't got nothink. 'E just fits ole Rogers's programme.

"And now I come to one of the bright spots of the ole thing wot you won't 'ardly believe in. Rogers's wife never knew nothink of wot 'er 'usband was up to. Not a word. She's as nice an old lady as ever you can meet. I'm afraid all this is going to be a narsty shock for 'er. A narsty shock. But there you are. She really took to the young chap, and arfter a bit they decides to wot they call adopt 'im.

"In the meantime 'e's got a job again, just as ole Rogers meant 'im to, on boats going to South America. And every trip he makes 'e brings ole Rogers a packet or two of wot 'e thinks are lottery tickets. Clever, that was. Ole Rogers could tell the young chap that 'e must keep 'em out of sight of the Customs, without 'is knowing wot 'e really was carrying in. So it went on. A nice comfortable business wot brought in a couple of 'undred pounds a trip clear and easy. And it was Fairfax's job to take the stuff from ole Rogers and get rid of it in London, or wherever he did get rid of it. That's why they pretends to 'ate one another. They was 'and in glove—Fairfax coming down for the fishing, whenever young Rogers was on leave. Easy, wasn't it?"

Stute looked bored.

"All of a sudden, after five or six years of this, ole Rogers gets a surprise. An air-mail letter turns up from Buenos Aires—I suppose from someone 'e'd got out there. You remember you sent Galsworthy round to enquire about it and 'e said it come from young Rogers 'isself. Wot does this letter say? Why, that the Argentine police are on to these 'ere drugs, and next trip out are going to arrest young Rogers for carrying 'em.

"That was a narsty turn for the ole man. It meant 'is smuggling days was done. 'E warns Fairfax, and they decides they'll finish up arfter this lot for good. They've each made a nice little bit. Fairfax decides to 'op off abroad with 'is wife as soon as ever he'd got rid of the next lot, and I don't know what ole Rogers planned. I shouldn't be surprised if it was 'arf miserliness with 'im. 'E may 'ave started meaning to use the toot one day, when 'e'd given up the game, but I imagine 'e'd got more and more fond of money till there you are. It was the money itself 'e was arfter. Still, you can't tell.

"Wot was certain was that the game was up. Young Rogers would have to be persuaded to chuck 'is job, else they'd arrest 'im when 'e got back. And the two of them would retire.

"Meanwhile it so 'appened that that Smythe girl 'ad got the idea of writing to Mrs. Walker. She wanted to find out young Rogers's address, and get something out of 'im. I daresay there was a baby in it somewhere, and it may 'ave been 'is or may not. But she 'ad 'is letters to go on, and she meant to make 'im cough up. So she writes to tell 'im she's on the spot and wot's 'e going to do about it, otherwise she'll come over and see 'is uncle and aunt. 'E wasn't too pleased when 'e got the letter, but 'e 'ad a bit of money, and decided 'e'd settle 'er.

"''E was in love with that nice-looking young lady with the 'orrible mother," Beef went on to explain, "and if I knows anythink, she was in love with 'im. She knew all about this Smythe, but she didn't want 'er mother to know nothink of that. Wouldn't 'ave done at all. So they decided between 'em very likely that it should be 'ushed up. That was arfter 'e come 'ome— but I 'aven't got to that yet. 'Ere, Mr. Townsend, I wish you could tell this story for me. 'Tisn't 'arf difficult when it's got 'arf a dozen beginnings. 'Ow you can write 'em up I don't know. Still I'll do me best. We must go back to old Rogers when 'e got that letter saying they'd rumbled the drug game out in that place—wherever it was."

CHAPTER XXXII

"Buenos Aires?" I suggested.

"Ah—that's it," said Beef. "Well, when old Rogers got that letter 'e made up 'is mind to retire, as I've told you. Only 'is difficulty was seeing as young Rogers didn't go back on that boat. If that was to 'appen all 'is work would go for nothink. Young Rogers 'ud be arrested out there and say 'oo it was 'e was bringing them packets in for. So 'ole Rogers made up 'is mind that 'is adopted nephew shouldn't never go back to that country, wotever 'appened. 'E was going to persuade 'im friendly if 'e could, and if 'e couldn't, well, 'e'd do 'im in, that's all!"

"Do you mean to suggest, Sergeant, that the elder Rogers actually proposed to murder the younger?"

"That was 'is idea, sir."

"This is becoming fantastic. I'm afraid it's largely your fault, Townsend, that Beef is indulging in this sort of romance."

"Well let anyone finish," begged Beef. "I'm telling you wot 'appened first, and I'll give you my proof afterwards. Now I've told you that ole Rogers was clever. Clever as a waggonload of monkeys, 'e was. 'E wasn't the one to go an' get 'isself into trouble for murder, when 'e'd got all that money to think of. So 'e works it out ingenious. First of all, being a mean little bloke, 'e decides on poisoning as the best way. Then 'e schemes out 'ow 'e'll do it. 'E 'as to get 'old of the poison. And it's not so easy nowadays, not a poison like this 'ere cyanide of potassium. 'E reads up in a dictionary . . ."

"A dictionary?"

"You know. Encyclopædia. Very likely 'e went round to the public library. 'E reads up about this 'ere cyanide of potassium, and 'e finds it's used for electro-plating. Ah, 'e thinks, that's the tip. And 'e remembers that there's a metal workshop over at Claydon where they does electro-plating. So one fine day over 'e 'ops to Claydown, and goes into the nearest outfitters 'e can find to buy 'isself a suit of metal-worker's overalls. Easy that is. And there 'e is."

"Where?" asked Stute sceptically.

"Standing in the street in Claydown with a suit of overalls wrapped up in a parcel under 'is arm. Well, 'e puts 'em on. Goes in a public lavatory, I daresay, an' comes out with 'is overcoat an' jacket wrapped up instead. Then 'e walks off towards those metal works."

It seemed to me that it was about here that Stute began to show a real interest in the Sergeant's narrative.

"'E looks for a chemist round about there and finds one in the street round the corner. So 'e pops in and asks casual for some cyanide of potassium for the works. The chemist doesn't

know 'im, but 'e knows that they use the stuff
round there and supposes it'll be all right.
'E's never been asked from there before. If 'e'd
known a bit more about it 'e'd 'ave found out
that the works got it 'olesale from London, an'
kept it under lock an' key. But there you are.
'E saw this experienced-looking ole man come
in in his overalls as calm as you please an' say
'e'd come from the works. And 'e lets 'im 'ave
it, just as 'ole Rogers thort 'e would, and that's
that.

"Then the ole chap 'as the problem of the
overalls. 'E can't just leave 'em somewhere.
Wouldn't do. Might give rise to all sorts of
enquiries. So 'e takes them 'ome with 'im.
Per'aps 'e means to burn 'em. But when 'is
wife sees a parcel she's all for knowing wot's
in it. Well you know what they are? Are you
married, sir?"

Stute nodded.

"You know all about it then. 'Wotever
'ave you got there?' she asks. 'Oh nothing,
only a suit of overalls I bought as a present
for young Alan,' says ole Rogers. And she
keeps them put away for the chap when 'e
comes 'ome. Meanwhile the 'ole man's ready
for 'im. If 'e can persuade young Rogers to
chuck up 'is job, marry that nice young lady,
and settle down, it's all right. If 'e can't, well,
'e's got the means to see 'e never goes back to
where' they'd arrest 'im. And 'e waits for 'im
to come on leave. 'Ave you got the right
time, Mr. Townsend?"

"It's nearly ten," I said.

Beef sighed. "Ah well," he said, "duty first. I'll tell you the rest of it now I've begun. Young Rogers comes 'ome. But that foreign-looking chap's been a shaddering of 'im day and night. . . ."

"Day and night?" said Stute.

"You know wot I mean, sir. They meant to find out wot 'e was up to. They're artful, those foreign police. They wanted all the credit for the job. They weren't going to let on to us that they knew about young Rogers. Not them. They sends a man 'ome on his boat to see wot 'e gets up to in England. And I for one aren't sorry that the man nearly got froze to death. 'Owever, young Rogers 'ad noticed 'im, and mentions it to 'is young lady.

"Then there's another thing. This 'ere Smythe's letter's waiting for 'im. One way and another it don't look like being much of a leave for 'im. But wot does 'e care? 'E's got a young lady and that's all 'e worries about. 'E tells 'er about this Smythe and decides to go over there on the Wednesday to settle 'er.

"Meanwhile Fairfax, 'oo young Rogers only knows as a gent wot comes down for the fishing, asks 'im to lunch at that private 'otel, and 'e can't do nothing but accept. So 'e sets out early for Chopley to see this 'ere Smythe, and when 'e gets there 'e's told she's not up yet. So 'e says 'e'll come back in the afternoon, after 'e's 'ad lunch with Fairfax and before 'e sees 'is young lady at seven o'clock. So far so good.

"Then this Fairfax gets on to 'im to leave 'is job. Old Rogers 'as already done all 'e can, but it won't work. Young Rogers is an independent sort of chap, and wants to get married. So 'e won't take no notice of either of 'em. 'E's earning good money, and 'e'll save enough to be able to tell 'is young lady's mother where she gets off. And 'e won't fall for no persuasion.

"After lunch 'e and Fairfax walk round to the Mitre for a drink, the ole person wot keeps the Riverside not even 'aving applied for a licence. While they're in there 'oo should come in but that foreign detective snooping about after Rogers. But when Fairfax sees 'im 'e knows the game's up. 'E clears off on the 2.50 train, and decides to 'op it for abroad with 'is wife next morning.

"Meanwhile, as we know, young Rogers 'as gone over to Chopley and seen Smythe. 'E pays 'er over what they arrange and she gives 'im 'is letters back. 'E wants 'er out of the districk as soon as possible, and offers to take 'er over for the six o'clock, to which she agrees. On the way he thinks 'e better not come 'ome with those letters, and 'e stops to burn 'em, which 'e does so careful that only that little bit of one was found by that Smith, of Chopley. But 'e doesn't want to be seen careering about Braxham with Smythe on the back of 'is bike, nor yet to 'ave to pass twenty minutes with her while they're waiting for the train. So 'e stops just outside, an' when 'e sees Meadows coming along 'e asks the exact time of the train. Then when it's just on time 'e runs 'er up to the station an' off she goes.

"Well, there's nearly an hour before 'e 'as to meet his young lady, so 'e stops at the Dragon for a drink, leaving 'is bike in the alley at the side. Then when 'e sees it's time for 'im to go 'ome and get ready, 'e's off again, and gets back to the shop between 'arf past six and ten to seven.

"Meanwhile 'is benevolent ole uncle 'as got everythink ready. 'E's seen it's no good trying to persuade young Rogers not to go back, so 'e's decided wot 'e'll do. In the first place 'e's arranged for 'is wife to be out of the way. And 'ere we come to somethink on which I can't see the truth for certain. Did those Fairfaxes know 'e had plotted to do in young Rogers or didn't they? I don't know. P'raps it'll come out later. Anyway, Mrs. Fairfax 'ad 'ad 'er instructions to keep ole Mrs. Rogers out of the way. She may not 'ave known why she 'ad to do it—or she may 'ave. But she succeeded. The poor lady never 'ad much fun, and when this Mrs. Fairfax suggested they should go to a music-'all she was on. So she was out of the way all right.

"When young Rogers gets round to the shop 'e found ole Rogers waiting for 'im. 'Your young lady's just been in,' 'e says, lying, as we *very* well know, 'to say she can't meet you to-night. 'Er mother won't let 'er out of the 'ouse.' And perhaps 'e goes on to say she'll meet 'im at a certain time to-morrow, or somethink of the sort. 'E doesn't want his nephew to go out looking for 'er, see, so 'e 'as to make it nice an' definite.

"Young Rogers is disappointed. More'n that 'e's bored. It's a rainy evening, and 'ere 'e is, stuck in with nothink to do. That's just wot ole Rogers wants. 'E starts up on a subject wot's 'e been 'ammering at for a long time. ''Ere,' 'e says, 'd'you want to get your own back on that Sergeant Beef?' he asks. 'I don't mind if I do,' says young Rogers, 'oo, as *we* know from others, 'as that very idea on 'is mind. 'I'll tell you just 'ow you can do it,' says ole Rogers, and they 'ave a drink together.

"'Is idea wasn't harf a clever one. 'Go an' tell 'im you've committed a murder,' 'e says. 'Committed a murder?' asks young Rogers. 'That's it. 'E thinks 'isself clever at murders ever since 'e found out about that last one. And 'e'll be off after this like lightening. Before you know where you are 'e'll 'ave Scotland Yard on it. Then see wot 'appens to 'im when they find 'e's brought them down on a wild goose chase.' Young Rogers likes the idea but doesn't see 'ow 'e's going to pull it off. 'But suppose 'e asks 'oo I've murdered?' 'e says to 'is uncle, an' a natural enough question when you comes to think of it. 'You won't be there to answer,' says 'is uncle, 'because when you've told 'im you've committed a murder you're going to pretend to commit suicide.' 'Ow's that?' asks young Rogers. 'Why,' says the ole man, 'we'll put some of my sleeping mixture in a bottle marked poison, and you'll swaller it quick, and pretend to go out. Then you'll go orf to sleep and they'll think you're drugged, with wot you've took, and Beef'll be on the 'phone to Scotland Yard in no time.'

"Young Rogers liked the idea of making a fool of me. 'E never could get over my 'aving run 'im in last time 'e was 'ome. And it sounded easy enough. 'E knew I thought 'e was a bit of a wrong 'un, and 'e thort I'd fall for the idea of 'im 'aving done someone in as quick as anythink. So 'e agrees."

There was no doubt about Stute's interest now. He was leaning forward, listening to every word.

"I don't know where the ole man got the idea from, but it was clever. See, it was safe as 'ouses. 'Oo was going to think young Rogers 'ad been murdered when 'arf a dozen people 'ad actually seen 'im committing suicide? It couldn't 'ave been plainer. Then they rigs up 'is sleeve with a drop of blood which ole Rogers gets from cutting 'is finger or somethink, and sticks a knife in 'is pocket, and there you are. Only when they comes to fill the bottle marked poison, wot Rogers 'as probably washed out elaborate in front of 'is nephew, the ole chap pours in a solution of the cyanide of potassium instead.

"Round comes young Rogers to the Mitre where I 'appened to be for a few minutes, as you know. And 'e carries out 'is part of thet plot so convincing that both you an' me, Inspector, spent a week or two looking for 'oo 'e'd murdered before I tumbled to it that 'e 'adn't murdered no one, poor fellow, but 'e'd been done in 'isself by 'is wicked uncle. It was a good idea though, because anyone might easily never 'ave suspected nothink but plain suicide."

CHAPTER XXXIII

Stute said, very quietly, "And now your proofs, Sergeant?"

"I'll soon tell you them," he said, "an' I'll tell you 'ow I got on to the idea. It was that poison. See, I didn't know much about it, either. Ignorance was bliss, as you might say, for I went round to the Public Library like old Rogers 'ad very likely done, and read up about it. And when I saw it was used for electroplating it 'itched up in my mind with wot 'ad been puzzling me all along—them overalls. It came over me all of a sudden, like you said things never did come, Inspector, that the ole man 'ad bought them overalls not for 'is nephew but for 'isself, to get that poison with, and that give me the 'ole idea.

"But of course I shouldn't never 'ave been able to get the details in without you 'adn't followed up all those people the masterly way you did. Finding that Fairfax, for instance, through them moving-van people an' wot that parson told you—that was clever if you like. And 'ow would I ever 'ave known wot motive 'e could 'ave 'ad if you 'adn't got on to them foreign police and found out about the game 'e was up to with drugs an' that? And then you 'aving all the resources of Scotland Yard to set on the finding of that Smythe—it all 'elped.

No, I couldn't 'ave got nowhere without the scientific side of it all.

"But you was wanting proof. As soon as you came back to London, sir, I thought I'd give my idea a chance. So I slipped over to Claydown and 'ad a look at the chemists' shops. And sure enough the one nearest that metal workshop remembered 'is going there in 'is overalls arfter the poison. So there and then I rings up the metal works, and just as I thought they'd never so much as thought of sending out for anythink of that. They got it in big quantities from an 'olesale firm. It would 'ave been out of the question for one of their men to go round. Of course, the chemist's in a fine old state. Well, I suppose 'e will get into trouble. I mean 'e ought never to 'ave served 'im without knowing 'oo 'e was. Still, you can understand it, with those overalls and that.

"Besides, I showed the chemist a photograph of old Rogers wot my h'excellent young constable, Galsworthy, 'ad taken. One of 'is 'obbies is photography, and 'e likes to 'ave a snap of anyone in the place wot we've got our eyes on. And ole Rogers being a teetotaller and a 'eavy church goer, we'd kept 'im under observation for a long time. So I 'ad his picture 'andy, and the chemist recognized it at once.

"Then I 'unted up the shop where he'd bought the overalls, and they remembered 'im, too. It was a dingy little place, and I should think they'd remember any customer as came in.

They certainly remembered 'im, an' I've got a note of their name in my book.

"Course, there's a lot more proof we shall get. There's 'is 'andwriting where 'e signed the poison book which I suppose some of your experts'll be able to swear was 'is, 'owever much 'e disguised it. And there'll be the Fairfaxes' word that the old man was in the drugs game, wot we'll be able to get out of them, easy enough, once they know we've got 'im. And there'll be Mrs. Fairfax's evidence that she was told to keep the old lady in London that night. And you'll soon 'ave all the details of 'is drug-selling.

"Then there's 'is running off. While I was waiting to see you just now, sir, I took the liberty of ringing up Galsworthy to see if 'e 'ad anythink to report. It appears that that chemist 'as been on the phone this afternoon. 'E says that about two o'clock someone rung 'im up at 'is' chemist's shop and pretended to be talking from Braxham Police Station. Asked if Sergeant Beef was there, or 'ad been in. The chemist, not thinking, said yes, this morning. Then afterwards when 'e'd gone over it in 'is mind, 'e thought it was funny anyone ringing 'im up like that, so 'e got on to Galsworthy to tell 'im. It was ole Rogers, of course. 'E'd 'eard I'd gone over to Claydown. . . ."

"I'm afraid that was my fault," I admitted. To tell the truth, I had been dreading the moment in which I should have to own to my indiscretion. "I mentioned to him where you had gone."

"That accounts for it then. 'E'd rung up, see, to find out whether I was on to 'im or not. If I wasn't—well, the chemist wouldn't think nothink of being asked polite whether I'd 'appened to've been in there. If I was on to 'im—well, 'e knew where 'e stood. So when the chemist said I 'ad been in, 'e pockets 'is 'undred quid, wot 'e always kept 'andy for an emergency, and 'eads off for the continent. But that's where we was too quick for 'im—Mr. Townsend and me. And 'e's safely in charge, and a good thing too."

The Sergeant stopped, and passed a large handkerchief over his forehead. He was beaming with pride and pleasure.

Stute was silent for thirty seconds or more.

"Well, Beef," he said at last, "I think you've hit it. In fact, in view of your chemist's evidence, I don't see that there can be much doubt. It's been a topsy-turvy case all through. It seems a bit absurd that your ignorance about cyanide of potassium should have put you on to something which I, with all the facts of the case at my disposal, missed. But I won't deny you followed it up well, and you're to be congratulated."

"Thank you, sir."

"The only thing is—I doubt if we could ever get a conviction for murder against old Rogers on the strength of this evidence, and I don't see how it can be improved in the necessary respect. We can prove that old Rogers bought the poison. But how are we to prove that he ever gave it to his nephew, or if he did so, that he made him think it wasn't poison? I'm afraid that if we were to bring such a charge the Judge would direct the Prosecution to reduce it to one of Being an Accessory Before the Fact of Felo de Se and for Aiding and Abetting Felo de Se."

"Oh no 'e wouldn't," said Beef, growing quite excited again, "I knew I was forgetting somethink! I've got a bit of evidence as 'ud put a stop to any of that wot you said, and show it was right down murder."

"Really? What is that?" The scepticism had quite gone out of Stute's voice, and he treated the Sergeant almost with respect.

"Why, when I went over to Claydown I 'ad another object in view. I was going to see Mr. Sawyer's brother, wot 'ad disappeared an' turned up again, and wot you laughed about when I told you. Well, I did see 'im, poor chap. 'E couldn't even come out an' 'ave one with me, in case 'is wife got to know of it. But 'e told me what she'd forbidden 'im to tell anyone, for fear of 'im getting mixed up in a case of murder an' that. Wot you didn't seem to take much notice of, sir, was that 'e was in Braxham on that Wednesday evening. Anyone else in the town as 'ad seen or 'eard anythink would 'ave come forward, but 'e couldn't very well, because 'e was 'iding out of the way of 'is wife. And 'e did know somethink, too. He 'ad run into young Rogers a few minutes past eight, as young Rogers was coming round to the Mitre. They knew each other well through 'aving met time and again at the Dragon. So Sawyer's brother asks him where 'e's off to and 'e says to the Mitre, to see if Beef's there. So Sawyer's brother asks wot he wants Beef for, and 'e says 'e's going to get 'is own back at last. 'Ow's 'e going to do it? asks Sawyer's brother. So 'e grins an' says, come and see, 'e'll do it all right, the way 'is uncle's shown 'im. But Sawyer's brother can't wait to see wot 'appens because 'e's got that wife be'ind 'im wot might start out in pursuit any minute, and then where'd 'e be? So 'e says good night, and off 'e goes, and young Rogers goes on to the Mitre. An' if that's not proof, I don't know wot is."

"Hm," said Stute, "that's better. Well, frankly, Sergeant, you've surprised me."

"I've surprised myself, sir. These things seem to come to me. I think I must 'ave been born for this business. You take that affair of when Mr. Larkin was finding discs in his cigarette machine every morning. . . ."

"Well, I don't think we'll go into that now, Beef. The point is that subject to confirmation of your facts you've succeeded where I . . . hadn't yet reached any conclusion. I don't think there will be much difficulty about charging Rogers. A very interesting scoundrel, and a very clever plot for murder. I shall give you full credit in my report, Beef. You may be lucky, but at any rate you are successful, and that's the important thing to us here. Anything more? Oh yes. Your notes. I see. Chemist's name and address. And so on. Good night then, Beef. Good night, Mr. Townsend. I suppose you'll be writing this up? I thought so. There's no crime nowadays without a novel, and very few novels without a crime. Good night to you both."

EPILOGUE

EPILOGUE

It was my last night in Braxham. In the noisy
heat of a crowded town hall I sat beside Sergeant Beef, waiting to see the final of the ——
shire Police Heavyweight Boxing Champion-
ships, in which P.C. "Chick" Galsworthy of
Braxham was to meet P.C. Theodore Smith, of
Chopley.

"I 'ope 'e'll win," said Beef for the fiftieth
time. "He deserves to, the way 'e's been training. Why, do you know, 'e 'asn't touched a
glass of beer for three weeks?"

"Yes. I hope he wins too," I said. "I never
cared for Smith. He was too anxious to please."

"You're right there," said Beef. "Well, we
shall see."

There were deafening shouts when Galsworthy,
looking very fit and fine, entered the ring, followed soon after by Smith. The latter looked
the more powerful man, his shoulders sloped
downwards as though under a great weight of
muscle, but Galsworthy, I thought, had the
more perfect physique.

I shall not describe that long and arduous
fight. This is not the place, and I am not the
man, to do so. I have never admired your
great detective's biographer who becomes side-
tracked by his ambition to display the width of
his interests. It is my job to chronicle the
triumphs of Sergeant Beef, not of his assistant.

Between the rounds Beef made elaborate
attempts at conversation. For a time the fight
went evenly enough and I think the Sergeant's
anxiety made him ape indifference.

"You know, Mr. Townsend," he said, as he
watched Galsworthy's seconds plying the towel
after the second round, "I've been talking
things over with Mrs. Beef. I've decided, if
they don't give me a job at the Yard after this,
I shall rest on my laurels."

"On your laurels?"

"I mean, I shall retire from the Force," said
Beef with great dignity.

Our conversation was interrupted by the bell,
and in this round it seemed that Smith had a
distinct advantage. He attacked most of the
time, and though Galsworthy's defence was
adequate for the most part, he took some
punishment before the round finished.

Beef seemed even more anxious to talk of
other things.

"But what makes you think there's any
chance of your being transferred to the Yard?"
I asked, rather amused at the idea.

"I think I've every right to it," exclaimed Beef.
"After all, I do find the answer, don't I?"

"You did this time," I said a little guardedly.

"Well. There you are. And if I don't get
my reward I shall retire altogether."

Once more the boxers were up, this time
Galsworthy started well, leading with his fav
ourite straight left. But at the end of the round
the position was uncertain.

"Then you'll give up detection?" I said with

some anxiety, fearing that a source of income to me would dry up.

"Not at all," said Beef. "I shall start on my own."

The idea of the Sergeant as a private investigator was even more startling than that of him as an Inspector at Scotland Yard.

"Good heavens," I said.

"Yes. That's wot I shall do. And Mrs. Beef agrees with me."

The fifth round was a nerve-racking one as Galsworthy went down for six, and it really seemed that it would be hard for him to establish a win unless he could achieve a knock-out. There was a red swelling beside his eye. After it Beef turned to me.

"I wonder," he said, "that you never 'ad a try to get yourself engaged to that nice young lady wot was gone on young Rogers."

I smiled. "You should be the last to complain," I said. "The day I become engaged I lose half my value as your companion in investigation. I should never be able to provide the love interest in the story again."

Beef nodded solemnly. "Perhaps you're right," he said.

In this round happened what was wholly unexpected to the spectators, though it has long been anticipated, I daresay, by readers of this tale. Galsworthy, with a heroic straight left, knocked out Smith, and was announced as winner of the championship.

But all that Beef allowed himself to say as we left the hall was—"Well, I'm glad 'e won."

"By the way, Sergeant, there's one way in which you deceived me. You told me, when you wanted me to charge old Rogers with theft, that life or death depended on it."

"Well? Didn't it? Didn't it make the difference of life or death to ole Rogers?"

He was quite right, I suppose. For the man was hanged soon afterwards.

THE END